Michael Hardcastle

The Team that
Wouldn't Give In

Illustrated by Trevor Parkin

Everything seems to be against Darton
United. They lose every game they play.
Ian, Damian and Alex rally together to try
to change the luck of the team but things
seem to go from bad to worse. It looks as if
United may be relegated from the Sunday
Junior League.

But nobody can say Darton United aren't
keen. At last the three friends have an idea
which gives the team a break.

MICHAEL HARDCASTLE

The Team that Wouldn't Give In

MAMMOTH

Also available by Michael Hardcastle in Mammoth

AWAY FROM HOME
CAUGHT OUT
FAST FROM THE GATE
FREE KICK
GREEN MACHINE
HALF A TEAM
IN THE NET
MASCOT
RIVAL GAMES
ROAR TO VICTORY
THE SATURDAY HORSE
THE SHOOTERS
SOCCER SPECIAL
THE SWITCH HORSE
TIGER OF THE TRACK
UNITED!
WINNING RIDER

First published in 1984 by Methuen Children's Books Ltd
Magnet edition published 1985
Published 1990 by Mammoth
an imprint of Mandarin Paperbacks
Michelin House, 81 Fulham Road, London SW3 6RB
Reprinted 1991

Mandarin is an imprint of the Octopus Publishing Group,
a division of Reed International Books Limited

Text copyright © 1984 by Michael Hardcastle
Illustrations copyright © 1984 by Trevor Parkin

ISBN 0 7497 0556 6

A CIP catalogue record for this title
is available from the British Library

Printed in Great Britain
by Cox & Wyman Ltd, Reading

One

Damian Tennant watched glumly as the opposition's centre-forward danced back to the centre circle in triumph after scoring his side's seventh goal. He ought, he knew, to feel anger at the way the goal had been given away by feeble defensive work. Instead, he simply felt numb. Behind Damian the goalkeeper, Davey Scott, fished the ball out of the net and punted it towards the middle. He exchanged shrugs with one of his full-backs but neither of them bothered to say anything. With another big defeat looming for Darton United there really was nothing to say that hadn't been said before, many times.

Almost reluctantly, Damian made his way back to his midfield position for the kick-off. There were times when he wished he'd never heard of Darton United or pulled on the team's green shirt and yellow shorts. This was definitely one of those times. With only ten minutes of normal time remaining there was no way in which United were going to salvage anything from this Sunday League match. Admittedly, a couple of goals from their strikers would help to improve the score-line; but, from the way they were playing, it was obvious that the forwards were in no better form than the defenders. So far Burnwood's goalkeeper hadn't had a real shot to save. It was no wonder that, at one point, a supporter had given him an anorak to help keep out the cold.

When the ball was pushed back to him, Damian decided to try a solo run. Probably he wouldn't get very far but at least it was a *positive* move and he would get some satisfaction out of it. He was supposed to remain in midfield to help try and stem the red tide of Burnwood attackers. However, he'd heard a top professional say on television that the best way to defend was to start an attack. Now Damian was about to put that theory to the test.

With the ball at his feet he suddenly surged forward and over the halfway line, taking two opponents completely by surprise because so far they'd seen him only as a central defender. Damian cleverly changed pace to outwit a Burnwood midfielder and the ease with which he made progress was an inspiration. Neil Dallimore, United's gangling striker, galloped ahead of him with renewed purpose and then called for a pass.

In United's three previous attacks – and there had been only three in the entire game – Neil had contrived to miss an open goal when a defender miskicked and then almost sprain an ankle when he clumsily trod on the ball. United could well do without another Dallimore disaster. So Damian ignored his team-mate and swerved towards the touch-line, thus surprising friend and foe alike. Nobody had the foggiest idea what he would do next, Damian included. On the other hand, he was still in possession of the ball and by now well into Burnwood's half of the field. At long last, he felt, Darton United were putting the opposition under real pressure.

Apart from Neil, no other Darton player had moved up in support of his run, as Damian quickly realised. That wasn't surprising. He and his team-mates were accustomed to spending the majority of their time penned in their own half with only the occasional fierce clearance to relieve the pressure on them. Fortunately, though, the Burnwood side were as baffled as everyone else by Damian's move and so no one tried very hard to tackle him. The nearest players simply stood off, waiting to see what he might try next.

The game appeared to have come to a halt. Then, losing patience, the Burnwood skipper rushed across, determined to get the ball. Skilfully, Damian dragged the ball to one side and out of anyone else's reach before darting forward again. As another opponent lumbered across his path, Damian deliberately flicked the ball against the boy's legs and then collected the rebound. The trick that he'd long wanted to try had worked beautifully. Suddenly, he was on the edge of the penalty area.

'It's a one-two, Neil!' he yelled to the willowy centre-forward as he drove the ball across to him and prayed for the instant return pass.

For once Dallimore played to instructions and the ball came back into Damian's stride. After so much inactivity the goalkeeper couldn't make up his mind whether to come out or stay on his line. It didn't matter to Damian what the goalie did. With the net in his sights he hit the ball with all the power he could muster.

Unhappily for him and United, his foot was under the ball rather than over it at the moment of contact. So his shot was still rising as it zoomed over the crossbar. The goalie's anxious expression switched to a smile.

'That was a really good move and a good run of yours, son,' murmured the referee as he came alongside Damian while running backwards to the halfway line. 'Next time just try to keep your shot down and then you'll really hit the net.'

Those were the most encouraging words about his football that Damian had heard for a very long time. He could sense that the referee wasn't just speaking out of sympathy for Darton's present plight.

For a few moments the United players responded to Damian's enterprise by tackling and kicking with zest. Billy Sandford, their skipper, actually began to yell enthusiastically to drive them on to new heights. For once he delivered a splendid pass for Neil to run on to – and Neil, still glowing from his successful exchange with Damian, tried to repeat that feat. This time, however, a Burnwood ball-winner felled Damian instantly with a crunching tackle.

That tackle was from behind and while the offender's name went into the referee's notebook the victim painfully got to his feet. It was one of those moments when Damian wished they had a trainer with a magic sponge (or, at the very least, a pain-killing spray). But even Mr Sandford, who liked to describe himself as United's manager, wasn't present at this match. Ruefully Damian rolled down his sock and rubbed at the scraped skin above the ankle. Undoubtedly he'd have a champion bruise there in the morning.

The game had to go on and he hurried to take up a good position for the free kick on the edge of the box. Billy, trying to assume a professional air as he realised the importance of this kick, flighted the ball well.

Although not very tall, Damian had strong legs and could jump to an impressive height. With his back to the goal, he met the ball perfectly with his forehead and glanced it down and sideways. Dalli-more was in just the right position to take advantage of such skill. But instead of picking his spot and coolly slotting the ball into the net he lunged at it

– and inevitably ballooned it over the bar to the delight of the stationary Burnwood defenders.

After that rare burst of excitement among the attacking force, the United team were unable to achieve any more near-triumphs before the final whistle shrilled. In fact, with thirty seconds to go they conceded another goal when Davey Scott fumbled a hopeful long shot from a Burnwood player who was simply trying his luck. Davey immediately explained to his pal, the full-back, that he'd let the shot in only because his hands were so cold because he hadn't touched the ball for a long time! 'Rotten luck, Davey,' said the full-back, and meant it.

Nonetheless, several of the team appeared quite cheerful as they trooped off the field and Billy Sandford was one of them.

'Well, not too bad this week, lads,' he announced to all who would listen to him. 'Kept the opposition down to single figures, didn't we? So we must have played twice as well as we did last week against Warton. Pity Dad wasn't here to watch us in this form.'

'Away scouting for some new players, was he?' asked Davey Scott with a perfectly straight face. 'I mean, we could do with one or two, couldn't we?'

'Like a new goalkeeper, for instance,' suggested Neil Dallimore, grinning at his own humour.

'Look, you weren't so good when you were the goalie, Dally-a-lot,' Davey snapped back at him. 'You were in goal when we had that record defeat

and so you were the one that let in 28 goals. That's twice as bad as I've ever done. So you have no room at all to talk.'

By the time they reached the dressing-room the argument between the pair of them was still going strong. Davey was repeatedly pointing out that if the so-called strikers would score a few then he, as goalkeeper, wouldn't be under so much pressure throughout the match – and, also, the score-line would look a lot better. Anyway, he concluded forcefully, it would soon be his turn to figure in the forward line and he would show them all how to find the net.

'I think we should stop changing our goalkeeper at regular intervals,' Damian announced as he sat on the bench to remove his boots and socks. He leaned his back against the wooden wall and looked around at his team-mates to see what effect his words were having on each of them. 'You can't take any pride in a job if you know it's not going to last very long. In this team I don't think we've got enough pride – and we ought to have *lots* of pride.'

'You're only saying that because it'll soon be your turn to go in goal,' Davey said quickly, his eyes narrowing with worry. 'Anyway, why should *you* miss out on the toughest job in the team?'

'I'm not trying to miss out on anything,' was the mild reply. 'But, in any case, I'm not really tall enough to be in goal, so – '

'Height doesn't really matter,' Davey cut in anxiously. 'It's all about being willing to throw yourself around and dive in among the flying boots where it hurts. That's what counts. My dad's mate is a goalie and that's what he says and he should know, shouldn't he? Oh, and he's not tall, either.'

'All I'm saying, really, is that we should stop switching around and try to become *specialists* in whatever positions we play,' Damian explained. 'We're bound to become better players if we concentrate on our own skills. If we improve as individuals we're bound to improve as a team. I mean, that's totally logical, isn't it?'

'My dad says all soccer players should be versatile and that's why he wants us to play in different positions,' Billy Sandford pointed out heavily. 'He's the manager so what he says goes. O.K.? You're not the captain, Damian, so I think you should shut up about tactics. You wouldn't be talking like that if dad was here in this dressing-room now.'

'So where is our manager today, then?' inquired Paul Merchant, who used to be a winger but had been converted into the team's sweeper by Mr Sandford. 'He was supposed to be telling me after this match whether I could go back to being a forward. He knows I'm not happy at the back. Come on, Billy, tell us why he isn't here.'

'Er, he, er, he just couldn't get away,' was the hasty answer as Billy thrust one leg after the other into his jeans. 'You see, er, well, it was the only day he could do a full check on the car. The engine's been making some weird noises lately and he wants to find out if, er, well, if it's safe to go on driving it without ... without....'

His voice tailed away as he ran out of ideas. He wished somebody would help him out but no one spoke. To cover his embarrassment he bent down and began a search under the bench for his socks.

'I think Mr Sandford has gone out shooting rabbits,' announced Ian Venn, emerging suddenly from the showers where the streaming water had darkened his straw-coloured hair. 'When my dad went into the gunshop the other day Mr Sandford was just buying himself a rifle and telling the manager he was going to have a change of sport at weekends. I don't think he noticed my dad had come in because he didn't speak to him. Or maybe he just didn't want to admit he was so fed up with our team he was abandoning us.'

For a moment or two no one could think of an appropriate comment on that astonishing bit of news. Billy, now distinctly pink with embarrassment, continued to scrabble under the bench for the elusive socks. Ian himself, pausing only to see the effect of his words on his team-mates, returned to the hot water to complete his ablutions. One of the smallest but most determined players in the squad, he normally didn't say much at any time. Accordingly, when he made a pronouncement it was taken to be the truth.

'Maybe,' said Neil Dallimore very slowly, 'maybe we can find another manager, somebody with lots of ideas and, er, lots of faith in us.'

'Nobody will want to take us on, not with our sort of record,' Paul Merchant admitted. 'Anyway, managers who are any good at all always go to the best teams. They don't identify with failure.'

This time everybody tried not to look at Billy Sandford. Billy stayed where he was, still searching. He knew how fragile was his hold on the captaincy of Darton United. Desperately, though, he wanted to retain it.

'I suppose we could try and join other teams –

you know, those that haven't got a full squad,' Davey Scott murmured in a voice that couldn't disguise his doubts.

'No chance!' was Damian's crisp rejoinder to that. 'You should know the rules, Scottie. The League doesn't allow transfers in the middle of a season unless there's an emergency. That wouldn't apply to us just because our manager had packed it in.'

'Maybe *we* should pack it in ourselves and then we can have some *fun* on Sundays,' someone else suggested gloomily.

'No! We've got to stick together and help each other to get better,' said Ian, stepping out of the showers again and this time reaching for a towel. 'We can do it if we really, really try hard to improve.'

Vigorously he rubbed his hair dry and then glanced down at the United's skipper.

'By the way, Billy,' he said casually, 'your socks are where you always put 'em – stuck in your jacket pocket.'

Two

As he scraped the last spoonful of yogurt from the carton Damian studied the Redbourne Sunday League tables on the sports page of the *Echo*. Although it was the most depressing sight imaginable, and he really did want to read something else to cheer him up, his eyes kept straying back to the table that included the name of Darton United. Nobody would have to look hard to spot it. United were bottom of the table.

What was even worse, they so far hadn't won a single point, let alone a match. All ten games played had resulted in defeats, ranging from those that could simply be described as heavy to others that were more like burials. On average they'd conceded more than twelve goals per game ... and scored exactly one goal every other game. To take the analysis one stage further, those five goals credited to Darton United included two penalties and one own goal. So, looked at from the bleakest possible viewpoint, that meant that United had managed to score only two goals themselves from open play in more than ten hours of playing time.

Damian shuddered and pushed the yogurt carton to one side. He didn't like yogurt, anyway, and ate it only because it was an energy food. Reaching for the jar of clover honey, he spread some thickly on a slice of wholemeal toast. One bite of that and he began to feel better: only fractionally better but, still, better. Soon he might even start to enjoy his breakfast. He could, for instance, take some comfort from the fact that the team directly above United in the table, French Hill Eagles, were only one point better off.

True, the Eagles also had a superior record in the goals for and against columns; but if United could defeat them when they met the following month then there was a distinct possibility that Darton would start to climb up the table at last. What was needed was a new team spirit and all-out determination to overcome all the odds that seemed forever to be stacked against them. On the credit side, they possessed a couple of talented players in Ian Venn and Paul Merchant in addition to himself (and Damian was perfectly capable of making a realistic assessment of his own abilities at soccer as in other things). Davey Scott could be quite useful as a goalkeeper if only he could be persuaded to concentrate at all times and also exert himself when he had at least a thirty per cent chance of making a save.

Billy Sandford was useless as a captain but he could pass a ball and he packed a decent shot. If Mr Sandford really had decided to relinquish the managership of United then his son could easily be replaced as skipper. A majority vote among the rest of the players was all that was needed. So who should take over? Damian hadn't any doubt who'd get his vote. Ian Venn was a very positive player in everything he attempted and he would lead by example. The fact that he was so small shouldn't count against him: Ian was never afraid to speak up for himself and challenge anyone he thought might be in the wrong. So, if –

'Damian, what *are* you thinking about?' asked his mother, slicing through his theories like an axe. 'Honestly, you look as though you're contemplating the end of the world.'

'It's not quite as bad as that,' he conceded. 'But pretty serious, all the same.'

'Football, I suppose,' she said with a resigned air.

'Naturally. That's just about as serious as you can get – especially when you consider our position in the Sunday League. If we don't start to improve soon we've had it for good.' He paused briefly for dramatic effect. 'At the end of the season the bottom two teams are relegated from the League. And teams that do get kicked out hardly ever get back in again. New clubs are always queuing up for places and the Management Committee say it's their policy to give new blood a chance to circulate. You can read that in the League Handbook. So you can see why I'm worried.'

He handed her the folded *Echo*, indicating with a tip of a finger the plight of United.

'Yes, I do see,' said Mrs Tennant, looking and sounding suitably solemn. She always took his troubles seriously and gave whatever advice and assistance she could. On this occasion, however, she couldn't think of anything she might be able to do to help United. Their fate was surely in the hands – or perhaps the feet – of the players themselves.

'You wouldn't, I suppose, think of joining another team, Damian?' his mother asked hesitantly.

'No, certainly not! You know I've always said that loyalty is very, very important in any team. If we don't stick together we've no hope of fighting our way out of trouble – no hope at all.'

'Yes, I quite agree with that attitude, Damian. It's very commendable.' She smiled, glanced at the sports page again and then gently shook her head. 'Still – '

At that moment the telephone started to ring. Mrs Tennant got up from the table very quickly, looking relieved at the interruption. 'I'll get it. Finish your toast.'

A moment later she was back to announce that the call was for him.

'For me? But I never get telephone calls – well,

hardly ever. Who is it, Mum?'

'Your team-mate and equally devoted fan of United, Ian Venn. Says he has a most urgent matter to discuss with you. He was very polite, as usual.'

'Ian? But I was just thinking about him – you know, when you asked me about my thoughts. Hey, great minds think alike! But what does he want to talk about?'

His mother laughed. 'Don't ask me, ask Ian! I'm not surprised if there's been a bit of thought transference because I reckon you and Ian are two of a kind, a real pair.'

'Yes,' said Damian softly as he made his way to the telephone, 'I think we are.' That idea had never occurred to him before but now he recognised the truth in it.

'Listen, we've got to do something about United before it's too late,' Ian said in a brisk, businesslike manner. 'We can't hang around just hoping that someone will come along and save us. We've got to sort out our real problems and come up with a solution.'

'Hey, that's just what I was thinking while I was having breakfast,' exclaimed Damian, delighted by this further evidence of their shared outlook. 'In fact, I was just saying – '

'Yeah, but thinking's not enough, Damian,' interrupted Ian. 'We've got to *do* things. Take some action. That's why I've called you up because I'm organising a meeting this morning to plan our tactics – you know, a new approach to the way we play so that we start winning and get off the bottom of the table.'

'You mean a team meeting, with everyone there?'

'No, I don't! I mean just the best players – you and me and Paul Merchant and Alex Anson. When we've talked things out we can have a sort of training session to put our ideas into practice before telling the rest of the team what's got to be done. You know the Whitecliff camping site?'

'Is that the one near the old windmill, just off the Coastal Road?'

'That's it! Well, that's where we're going to meet. There won't be anybody up there now and there's a good sports area where we can do some ball work without being spied on. It's an ideal spot for us. Look, it's now 8.48. Can you get yourself up there by ten o'clock?'

'Er, yes, I expect so. Do you know if Paul and Alex will definitely be there?'

'Well, I rang you first, of course. But I know they're on our side so they'll get there somehow. O.K.?'

'O.K., Ian. See you.'

He returned to the kitchen looking well-pleased with himself and explained to his mother that he needed a lift if he was to get to the campsite by the appointed time. She was, he deduced, in a good mood that morning and so he was sure his plea would be answered.

'Well, as it happens, I am going to the shops, so I suppose I could drive round that way, even though it is a mighty detour,' she told him in a calculating way. 'But, in return, I want you to do something for me. You've been putting if off for ages but it needs doing before winter sets in: the front fence to be creosoted. By Monday morning, all right?'

Damian wrinkled his nose at the prospect but knew he was in no position to refuse. 'O.K., Mum, it's a deal. But if the smell of that stuff makes me violently sick all over – '

'That's enough! We've got an agreement, so stick to it. Now, if we're going to get to this secret meeting of yours in time, you'd better shoot upstairs and get yourself ready. Your car will be leaving in ten minutes.'

When Damian arrived at the camping site seagulls were swooping low over the sports area to catch chunks of bread being thrown upwards by Ian Venn and Alex Anson. He hadn't known that Alex was a keen ornithologist with a particular fondness for studying (and feeding, whenever possible) sea birds. A slimly-built boy of medium height with a rather dreamy manner, Alex normally played at full-back and his greatest asset, in Damian's opinion, was that he could kick equally well with either foot.

'I come up here quite a lot, mainly to watch

cormorants,' Alex explained when Damian said what a breezy spot it was. 'The air can be very invigorating. That's one of the reasons I suggested it to Ian as a suitable training ground. If you can control the ball up here in half a gale you can control it anywhere.'

'Have you two been planning this meeting for some time, then?' Damian asked.

'No, I only decided last night,' Ian replied. 'I just remembered what Alex had said when I realised we needed somewhere private. Oh good, here's Paul. Now we can get down to work.'

Paul, his round face beaming at the sight of them,

23

was the only one not in a tracksuit; and, he confessed, he wasn't even wearing his football shorts under his trousers.

'I didn't know we were going to have a kick-around,' he said guiltily. 'I thought we were just going to, you know, sort things out in a discussion.'

'I did explain on the phone that we were planning some ball work but I expect you weren't listening properly,' Ian pointed out. He smiled as he spoke, to take the sting out of the words, but it was still a reprimand.

'Sorry, Ian. Really I am. But I can still join in as I am, can't I? I mean, I often play at school like this. In fact, in break-time and lunch-time games I'm third top scorer! So ordinary trousers don't hold me back, you see.'

Ian nodded. Then, picking up his sports bag which contained a football as well as his boots, he led them across to a grassy mound overlooking the playing area. It was screened from the road by a row of bushes and so afforded them all the privacy they needed. From the way he began to talk, it was obvious to the other three that he had considered the background to United's plight very carefully before coming up with suggestions to improve matters. He stressed that they were only suggestions and that anyone was free to tell him that his ideas were crazy and couldn't possibly work; but if his listeners did agree with him then he hoped they could all act together to put them into operation. At the same time, he hoped that if anyone else had some good ideas they, too, could be discussed at this meeting.

'I've been thinking of some changes we ought to make,' Damian put in. 'But you go ahead. I expect we're working on the same lines.'

Ian exchanged glances with Alex and then said: 'Well, the first thing we've got to decide is who's going to be in charge of the team from now on. You see, after that shambles against Burnwood, I got Billy Sandford on his own and he confessed that his dad really has given up the manager's job. But he was too embarrassed to tell us himself, Billy says. Typical! I mean, he wasn't much good to us in any way, was he? Anyway, Billy wasn't going to say anything if he could avoid it because he wants to hang on to the captaincy. But he's useless, too: he couldn't lead a dog to a gate-post!'

They all laughed and no one disagreed with such a verdict.

'I've been analysing all the players and I think we're the only ones who can really run the team in the future,' continued Ian earnestly. 'So we should form ourselves into a committee and then find some adult to help us out with raising funds and taking us to matches when we have a long way to travel – that sort of thing. We need *somebody* who is really keen and organised and *believes* in us as a team that's going to get better. Won't be easy but we've got to start looking for a bloke like that.'

As he paused for breath, Damian quickly re-marked: 'You've said we need a new captain and I'm sure we all agree. Well, I think you should have the job, Ian.'

'I second that,' Alex said before anyone else could speak. Paul nodded vigorously.

'Well, I was going to suggest, you, Damian,' Ian disclosed.

'Damian can be the vice-captain,' was the next prompt response from Alex. 'We need a deputy if ever Ian has to miss a match. We don't want to give Billy a chance to creep back in. I'm sure the rest of the lads will support us.'

'Thanks very much for your confidence in me,' said Ian in a manner that suggested he was pleased with what had happened but that he hadn't ex-pected it. 'I'll do everything I can not to let United down. A cousin of mine – he's twelve years older than me – just might be able to help out on the management side. He's pretty keen on soccer and plays sometimes for a works' team. So I'll have a word with him next time he's at our place.

'But we've got to start putting some things right ourselves without wasting any more time. In my opinion, the first thing we've got to improve is our tackling.'

'Tackling?' queried Paul with obvious astonish-ment.

'Look, probably the chief reason why other teams walk all over us is that we don't tackle 'em properly when they've got the ball,' was Ian's emphatic reply. 'We just chicken out or something – or, as I think, our technique is wrong. We don't go in as hard and as direct as we should. We pussy-foot about and go in for half-hearted trips that just gets free kicks for the opposition. We've got to change all that, Paul.'

'But I'm really a winger, not a sweeper, as Mr Sandford made me last month. If I go back to being a forward then I don't have to bother about being a good tackler.'

Ian shook his head. 'Poor thinking, that, Paul. *Every* player has to learn how to tackle. Forwards should learn to tackle opposing forwards when necessary – and often forwards have to drop back to help out when their defence is under pressure. One of our weaknesses is that our forwards haven't helped out enough. They've stood around and done absolutely nothing at times.'

Paul really had no answer to that. In the past he himself had complained about team-mates not dropping back to become extra defenders when needed.

'If we can start winning the ball in one-to-one situations, especially in midfield, then we can start going forward in strength – midfielders alongside the forwards,' declared Alex, a light of endeavour in his grey eyes. 'I might even get into an attacking position myself!'

'Exactly! I'm sure that as soon as we start going

27

forward in strength, we'll start winning matches,' Ian agreed. 'Anyway, that's enough talking. Let's get on with some work on the ball. *Hard* work. We've got to master the ball-winning tackle ourselves before we can teach the rest of the team.'

The three who were wearing them stripped off their tracksuits, put on their boots and went through a few loosening-up exercises. A wind had got up while they talked and now there was a distinct chill in the air. They divided into pairs, Ian and Alex on one side, Damian and Paul on the other, so that they could practise passing and dribbling together as well as tackling. Damian had long regarded tackling as one of his own weaknesses but had done little to improve it; trouble was, he tended to think of himself as an attacking midfielder rather than as an extra defender.

'O.K., let's get on with the important thing,' called Ian when he decided they'd done enough to warm themselves up. 'Just remember this about the tackle: you've got to watch the ball, not the man. You won't get fooled by a swerve or a dribble if you keep your eye on the ball, not the player's feet. Right, you've got the ball, Damian. So you and Paul come at us and one of us'll take it off you. That's a promise!'

On their first attempt to get past the opposition, Damian and Paul succeeded easily because Alex was caught off balance by Damian's body swerve ('I told you to watch the *ball*,' Ian hissed at his partner); but the next time, Ian went in with a crunching tackle to take the ball off Paul's instep. Paul was so surprised that he stumbled and sat down.

'See what I mean?' Ian grinned. 'Total determination, that's the secret! You've got to believe you can't fail to win the ball. Now it's your turn. So, watch out, here we come!'

They moved forward at a brisk pace, switching the ball between them as rapidly as possible. Damian, who was directly facing him, was sure that Ian would retain possession at the critical moment. He eased back a step or so, trying to pick the perfect moment to go for the ball. Paul, equally keen to do well, was on Damian's left and now he moved closer to his fellow defender as if he knew for certain that Ian would hold on to the ball.

Suddenly, Ian swerved to his left and then appeared to hesitate, perhaps fearing that he hadn't got the ball under complete control. In that split-second Paul leapt forward. As he crashed bodily into his opponent his right foot came down heavily on Ian's left leg, just above the ankle.

The sound that they all heard was like the crack of a rifle.

Three

For all his clumsiness in the collision, Paul Merchant was quick to get to his feet. He had fallen across Ian Venn and his first thought was to help his victim to get up.

'No! Leave him where he is,' Damian ordered fiercely as he saw Paul reach out for Ian's hand.

One look at Ian's face, contorted with pain, was enough to tell him how bad the injury might be. He glanced down at Ian's legs and saw that there appeared to be a bulge above the ankle on the left one: and Ian wasn't wearing shinpads under his long socks. Although he'd never seen one before, he felt certain that Ian's leg was broken. The noise they'd heard was of the bone snapping.

Ian's face was as white as his shorts when Damian bent over him to ask how he felt. Even though his eyes seemed to be drowning in tears, Ian still managed to sound as calm as ever when he spoke.

'The pain's pretty bad. In my left leg. I think – I think I must have broken it, Damian. I daren't try

31

to – to move it.'

Paul was kneeling beside them, desperate to be believed as he repeated over and over again that it had been an accident, that he'd do anything, if only he knew what to do, to make up for his stupidity. Alex, meanwhile, was fetching his anorak to put over Ian to keep him warm.

'I could do with a drink, more than anything,' Ian gasped. 'I'm feeling a bit odd, my head's a bit swimmy.'

'No drink,' said Damian crisply. 'The, er, hospital wouldn't want you to have one before they, er, look at you. Look, Ian, we've got to get help. I'm going to ring for an ambulance – dial 999. They'll be getting here in no time, I expect. You won't have long to wait, I promise.'

He sensed that Ian was listening though now his eyes were closed and he seemed to be sweating; even his hand felt clammy. Damian, who'd once read a book about sports injuries, guessed that United's new captain was in a state of shock because of the severity of his injury.

'I came up on my bike – you can borrow that, Damian,' Alex told him. 'There's a phone kiosk just down the coastal road in a lay-by. Oh yes – have you got some money? I think – '

'You don't have to pay for an emergency call. While I'm away you two keep Ian warm. That's vital. And don't move him, whatever you do. Oh, and thanks for the bike, Alex. Makes a lot of difference. O.K., I'll be back as soon as I can.'

As he built up speed across the camping area Damian prayed that the telephone would be in good working order, that it was one the vandals had missed. He knew that Ian needed to be treated in hospital without delay; probably he would have an anaesthetic so that the bone could be set and that was why he wouldn't be allowed anything to drink before the operation. Fervently he hoped that the break was a clean one; then, with a bit of luck, Ian would be playing soccer again before the season ended.

On such a normally deserted stretch of road, unbelievably, the phone box was occupied when he reached it. He propped the bike against the side of the kiosk and stalked round and round in sight of the man within; should he risk opening the door and pointing out that he wanted to dial 999? The steely look in the eye of the man when he caught sight of him was a deterrent. Undoubtedly he would a) tell Damian he was being impertinent; b) order him to be patient; or c) simply employ strong language. In fact when, half a minute later, he vacated the box it was with a friendly grin and the comment: 'All yours now, son.'

For the first time in his life Damian called the emergency number.

'Which service, please?' asked a cool, clear voice.

'Er, we need an ambulance. Soon as you can.'

There was a momentary hesitation and then the

voice inquired: 'Is this a genuine emergency? You sound very young. You can be in a lot of trouble if you make a hoax call, young man.'

'It IS an emergency! My friend's broken his leg. His name is Ian Venn and mine is Damian Tennant. We play for the same soccer team. Oh, please, hurry up. He's in a bad way and needs to get to hospital.'

This time there was no delay. A split-second after answering the operator's request for the location of the telephone box, he was put through to the ambulance station. They didn't doubt his word for a moment: as soon as they knew what had happened they promised instant action. An ambulance would be with them within minutes.

It was, too. Damian barely had time to check on Ian's progress during his absence before the ambulance, headlights blazing, blue light flashing, was sweeping into the camping ground, followed almost immediately by an equally frenzied police car. That was nothing to worry about, the police driver assured the boys, it was standard procedure for the nearest police vehicle to check out any emergency call for an ambulance.

With as much tenderness as speed, the ambulance attendants lifted Ian on to a stretcher after examining his leg. Before he disappeared from sight into the vehicle Ian somehow summoned up a wan smile. He murmured something but the boys couldn't catch his words.

'He was probably saying something about

34

United,' Alex explained to Damian. 'While you were phoning for the ambulance he kept saying that we must stick together. We must keep on playing whatever happens. He said when he's fit again he'll want his place back in the team.'

'You know,' said Damian softly, 'he'd have been a terrific captain. He's got real guts as well as talent.'

'Well, you've got to forget Ian for the time being,' Alex pointed out with unexpected candour. 'It'll be weeks before he's back playing for United. From next Sunday's match, *you* will be captaining the team.'

Four

Damian tried to quell his nervousness by imagining what the England manager would say in similar circumstances. Doubtless he would tell his players to go out there and do their best for their country; but, above all, they should enjoy themselves. If they were enjoying themselves then, automatically, it followed that they'd be playing well. Top managers were always saying things like that and, usually, their teams got good results. The only big difference, as far as he could tell, was that most managers remained on the bench throughout the match whereas he, Damian, would actually be out on the pitch, playing in the match.

He glanced round the rickety dressing-room, with its scarred walls and broken clothes-hooks, licked his lips and launched into his first ever pep talk as captain of Darton United.

'Look, I'm really grateful to you all for agreeing that I should be captain and I'll do my very best for you – for United – at all times,' he began. He knew that he was speaking much too fast but that didn't matter as long as they got the message: and it was gratifying to see that most of them were listening intently. 'But personalities aren't as important as the team itself. We've got to go out there and play as a team, with everyone helping everyone else. It doesn't matter who scores the goals, or makes fantastic saves at the other end. The only important thing is doing well as a team.'

Damian paused to see if anyone wanted to make a comment but they all appeared to have been struck dumb.

He resumed: 'O.K., we've had some horrific results in the last few weeks, I know. But we've got to forget them and think only about the future. We've got a new spirit in the side from today and we must make it work for us.' At that point he couldn't resist glancing directly at Billy Sandford, the deposed captain. Billy, however, was apparently worried only about a hole in his left sock. 'Well, we have a great chance to get off to a good start. Turnbridge Rovers aren't a good team. That's why they're in the middle of the table because they aren't anything special. No hopes of promotion, no worries about relegation. We should be able to beat them because they're not ambitious and we are. So, lads, let's get out there and show 'em. Let's give 'em a few big surprises.'

As they reached the playing area Alex Anson moved alongside Damian for a quiet word. 'You did that well, skipper. I think they've got the message. Remember, I'm always ready to help you in any way.'

Damian was greatly impressed by the support he'd already received from the full-back. He hadn't realised what an ambitious boy Alex was but as soon as Damian had suggested he should be the new vice-captain Alex accepted with alacrity. What's more he'd taken the leading role in persuading the rest of the players to vote for Damian as the new skipper. Billy hadn't objected too strongly because he knew he was in a weak position in the absence of his father; and, anyway, he wanted to keep his place in the side. Alex said little but he didn't hesitate to act. One of his first self-imposed tasks had been to find a new player for United. He had chosen one of his school friends, Jonathan McGuigan, who hadn't played regularly for a team at any level. Jonathan, tall and strongly built, was a natural left-footer and that alone was a bonus to United.

No sooner had Damian joined in the shooting-into-goal kick-about than he was being summoned to the centre circle by the referee to toss up with his rival for choice of ends. Damian correctly called heads – that alone seemed a good omen – and decided that United would play with the slope in their favour. It wasn't a severe gradient but the tilt was towards one corner flag, which made things difficult sometimes for wingers.

'There's one thing I want to stress to you both,' the referee told the captains. 'I won't stand for any bad behaviour, not by anyone. Bad sportsmanship will be dealt with in the strictest fashion. Understood?'

They nodded – and then, when the referee turned away to whistle up the rest of the players, they exchanged conspiratorial winks. Both knew their teams would play as they normally did whatever anyone said before the match began.

In their smart black-and-white striped shirts, black shorts, and scarlet socks Turnbridge Rovers didn't look like a team without ambition – and they didn't start like one, either. From the kick-off they kept possession very skilfully with their strikers exchanging one-twos at bewildering speed. Then, in a sudden change of direction, the ball was driven out to the right flank. Alex Anson rushed across to make a tackle but slipped on the greasy surface and simply slid humiliatingly into touch, on his back.

Without hesitation, the winger crossed the ball into the front area of the box. Davey Scott jumped up and down on his line but didn't come out; it wasn't really a goalkeeper's ball. But Paul Merchant didn't agree with that viewpoint. Fiercely he yelled at Davey to 'come out and grab it!'

Paul should have gone for the ball himself and the delay was fatal. Rovers' centre-forward, who had started the entire movement, nipped past the stationary defender, took the ball under control, moved on a couple of paces and then fired it home to the goalkeeper's right.

Turnbridge had scored the first goal in thirteen seconds without a United player so much as getting a touch of the ball. Darton's defence had instantaneously proved to be just as feeble as its goals-against record suggested. Rovers, having tasted sweet success so swiftly, were now determined to make the most of it.

'What were you *doing*, standing there like a dummy?' Paul demanded of the goalkeeper. 'You just handed that goal to 'em on a plate, Scottie. You're as useless as ever.'

Davey was furious. He'd only agreed to remain in goal for the next couple of matches because Damian and Alex had been so flattering and persuasive. Rovers' goal, he knew very well, was not his fault but Paul's. He'd never liked Paul and always regarded him as a trouble-maker.

'Don't you talk to me like that,' he yelled as he rushed from his net towards Paul, on whose face he detected a sneer. Well, he'd wipe that off for a start. Without another moment's thought, Davey swung his right fist.

As so often was the case when he tried to punch the ball clear, he missed his target. But he struck Paul on the collar-bone: and Paul, as much through surprise as the force of the blow, fell flat on his back.

The referee, who'd been about to re-start the

game, had a clear view of the incident. At top speed he tore up the field to administer justice and, simultaneously, set an example to the other ruffians in the United team (as he assumed them to be on this evidence).

'We're not having that!' he thundered at Davey Scott, now utterly astonished at his own conduct and the outcome of it. 'If you can attack one of your own players like that what on earth would you do to the opposition? I dread to think. But you're not going to have the chance – oh no. Leave the field immediately! But take off your jersey first. Another player is going to need it, unless your team intends to continue without a goalkeeper.'

Damian sprinted up to see what salvage work he could carry out. By now, Paul had picked himself up, totally unscathed, and avoided Damian's eye. He had wanted to return to being a winger instead of acting as sweeper but had agreed to play on at the back to please his new captain. After what he'd done to Ian he could hardly dictate his own terms.

'Can't you give him another chance, please?' Damian politely asked the referee. 'I'm sure it was all a mistake. It'll be very difficult for us without a proper goalkeeper.'

'That should have been thought of before this hooligan was selected for your team,' was the official's unbending attitude. 'Now hurry up and decide who is to wear the green jersey. We've been held up long enough by bad conduct. Oh yes, and

you should understand that I won't hesitate to re-move other offenders from the field if anything like that occurs again. You must learn to control your players.'

It had never occurred to United's new skipper that he should have a replacement goalkeeper in mind in case of emergency. However, as he glanced round at his players to make a choice, a volunteer stepped forward.

'I don't mind having a go if you like,' said Jonathan McGuigan. 'I used to play in goal often at my previous school.'

'Oh, great – thanks,' replied a relieved Damian. 'I'll have to keep my fingers crossed and hope we don't get any injuries. Honestly, I think there's a jinx on this team. But good luck with the saves, Jonathan.'

As if to prove that he had skills the equal of any Turnbridge players, Neil Dallimore made a supreme effort to keep the ball from the kick-off. The gangling striker went weaving across the centre-circle and into the heart of Rovers' midfield. After half-stumbling over his own feet, Neil dribbled past one player and then was brought to the ground by a sliding tackle. At the very least, that should have brought a warning to the Turnbridge offender but the referee just flapped his arms to indicate they should play on.

Damian's heart sank a little lower. It didn't need a genius to work out that this wasn't going to be

United's day.

With United down to ten boys the skipper him-self had to drop back deep into defence. Addi-tionally he needed to give support to Paul, still shaken by being the unwitting cause of Davey's dismissal. Even so, they weren't, between them, able to prevent Rovers scoring again. Elated by that instant success, their strikers combined fluently when the ball reached them and this time the pro-gress was down the left flank. Then, with a neat change of direction, the ball was hooked into the middle. The centre-forward chested it down, beat off a challenge and aimed for the top of the net. And he found it – despite a quite heroic effort from Jonathan to tip the ball over the bar.

Damian wondered what he could do to stave off another crushing defeat for his side. They were so used to being overwhelmed that they'd almost lost the will to fight back. It could have been so different if they'd got off to a good start and proved they had the skill and enterprise to rattle the opposition. As it was they'd blundered into disaster in practically record time. His own stature as the new skipper would be meaningless unless United adopted a positive approach and at the very least created scoring chances for themselves.

Their first need was to keep possession: if they held on to the ball, instead of simply whacking it anywhere, then they had hopes of making progress. The captain himself ought to set the example and so, as soon as possible, Damian took command of the ball. The strength in his legs and his balance were great assets as he rode a couple of tackles and ploughed a diagonal course towards goal. Twice he faltered because of lunging challenges from Turn-bridge midfielders but he parted with the ball only on his own terms. He flicked it accurately to Billy Sandford with the instruction: 'Push it back, Billy, push it back!'

Billy did as he was told. The deposed skipper still feared that he might be left out of the team al-together and he was determined to avoid that fate. He wasn't sure what Damian had in mind but he respected his footballing ability as well as his intel-ligence. Mr Sandford had more than once remarked at home that young Tennant was 'the thinker' of the side.

Ignoring Neil Dallimore's frenzied screeches for a pass, Damian went off on a solo run in another direction. This time, Turnbridge defenders tended to stand off and wait for him to make a mistake. After all, he wasn't exactly heading for goal.

What Damian hadn't realised was that Rovers had instinctively relaxed. Their instant two-goal lead, coupled with Darton's abysmal playing re-cord, had convinced them the match would be a walk-over. They could probably score at will. Cer-tainly they didn't have to exert themselves. It was that sort of lazy attitude that kept them in the middle of the table. With the talents they possessed they ought really to have been pressing for promotion. Now their defenders expected Damian to run out of steam very quickly; in any case, he was going into no-man's-land near the corner flag – he was no threat at all because he was on his own. No other United player had thought to give him close support.

Damian suddenly had the impression that he was playing a game of his own. With no one to pass to, he had to turn and try a new path parallel with the dead-ball line. A full-back lumbered at him like an earth-mover but Damian simply jinked one way, then the other, and the full-back fell over his own studs. Then Damian spotted Stevie Pailthorp running through the middle towards the edge of the box. Officially, Stevie was United's right-winger but for some reason he'd hidden himself in midfield. He felt he was lucky to be in the team at all. Even he, however, recognised that he could run – and run fast.

'Yours, Stevie!' yelled Damian, sending him a long, and splendidly judged pass.

Stevie swooped on to the ball, pushed it forward for a couple of long paces, and then let fly with his right foot. He hit it beautifully, and he hit it with surprising power.

The ball appeared to be passing just over the crossbar when, without warning, it dipped and then buried itself in the top of the net – before gently falling to the ground behind the astounded goalkeeper.

For a few moments Damian was equally stupe-fied. He hadn't even expected Stevie to try a shot let alone score a goal. On the basis of the way he'd played in recent matches, who would have guessed he was capable of such enterprise? However, that didn't prevent his intoxicated team-mates from rushing up to pour congratulations all over him. It was only United's sixth goal of the season – and undeniably it was the best.

'I just thought I ought to test out their goalie – give 'em something to think about,' was Stevie's modest reaction to his success. 'I mean, Damian said we must attack whenever we had the chance.'

It was just the inspiration Darton needed. From then on there was real bite in their tackles, real purpose in their passing: the aimless kick in a scramble for the ball became a rarity. That 'thun-derbolt out of the blue', as their manager described it, didn't have a chastening effect on Rovers, after all. The players seemed to treat it as the sort of fluke that couldn't be repeated: and so they con-tinued with their casual approach to the game. They felt they could work their way into the United penalty area at will and so, when attacks broke down, they patiently waited for the opportunity to build another one.

All the time, Damian was shouting encourage-ment to his players, neglecting no one who made a firm tackle or an accurate pass. He even wondered if he was overdoing it but the important thing was to keep up their morale. In Mr Sandford's time as manager they scarcely ever heard a word of praise: sarcasm was the whip he kept cracking. The players hadn't responded very effectively to that so perhaps a different style of leadership was necessary.

The most heartening development was the display by their stand-in goalkeeper. Twice when Rovers broke through into the box, Jonathan McGuigan came off his line to foil them, diving bravely for the ball at the forwards' feet. On another occasion he palmed away a fierce shot with almost nonchalant ease. His height was an advantage but it was his competent handling that counted. If he were happy to continue in goal after this match then that would be a real bonus for United, Damian reflected.

Stevie, now that he was a hero, was doing all he could to become the first United player ever to score two goals in one match. Eagerly seeking the ball, at one point he even vied with a team-mate for possession so that he could launch, and participate in, another attack. His speed carried him past midfielders who had to turn but the Turnbridge left-back was a useful sprinter, too, and he was tending to shadow Stevie. During one raid Stevie insisted on trying to do everything himself when Neil Dallimore was screaming for a pass – and was in just the right position to make the most of it.

At half-time the score was still 2–1 to Rovers and

Damian could feel satisfied with that after such a dreadful start for United. The players didn't leave the field for the break but huddled in groups on opposite sides of the pitch. Alex Anson had thoughtfully provided a plastic bag containing oranges already cut in halves. That was more than Mr Sandford had done for them and the players gratefully sucked them dry as they listened to Damian's remarks. Much of the time he simply praised their performance. He couldn't think of any tactical changes they could, or ought to, make, apart from mentioning, as casually as possible, to Stevie that the attack might function better sometimes if he released the ball sooner when another forward was up with him.

'We can get a really good result from this match if we keep on playing in the same way,' he concluded as they were about to troop back on to the pitch. 'I told you Rovers weren't so great. Now I think we can prove we're the *better* team. So let's get at them right away.'

Not surprisingly, Turnbridge had been given a roasting by their manager at half-time and so they, too, were determined to resume at a scorching pace. Neil Dallimore blinked at the ferocious manner in which his opposite number hacked the ball away from him to set up the first attack. In what was almost a duplicate of the first move of the entire match, the ball was switched to the wing before being hooked cleverly into the penalty area. This time, though, Jonathan McGuigan reacted instantaneously. With bounding steps he came out, gathered the ball above his head as if removing an apple from a tree, dodged round an opponent and then hoofed the ball to his own right wing. He gave neutral observers the impression that he'd spent his life keeping goal.

Stevie combined neatly with Billy Sandford and, in the course of the next few minutes, United began to look at least the equal of their opponents. For the first time that he could remember Damian found that he had the time to play exactly as he wanted to: he was able to control the ball, look for an opening or a team-mate to pass to and generally run the game for his side. It became an exhilarating experience: and it was crowned by the equaliser.

Billy Sandford started the move just inside Rovers' half after picking up a sliced clearance. His long pass to Damian on the right was hit hard and true – and Damian outwitted his marker by side-footing the ball immediately to Stevie, who accelerated towards the box.

In his enthusiasm the speedy winger allowed the ball to run too far ahead of him. It was directly in the path of a defender and he should have dealt with it easily: instead he tried to boot it clear and missed his kick completely – and spectacularly. Somehow the ball caught the heel of his non-kicking foot, spun sideways and fell appetisingly in front of Neil, who'd sensibly made up a lot of ground in support. Even Dally-a-lot at his worst couldn't miss an open goal like that for the keeper was well out of position. Even so, Neil contrived to hit the ball against the inside of the far upright before it entered the net.

For the first time that season, Darton United had scored two goals in a game; even better, they were now on level terms with Rovers. Every single member of the team had a vision of United collecting their first League point.

'Hold on now, lads,' Damian urged his players. 'Don't let 'em get back into the game.'

While Rovers' defenders argued among themselves about who was really responsible for giving (as they saw it) United the equaliser, their forwards battled furiously to regain a winning position. The manager's fevered orders to 'knock the ball about and stretch their defence' were obeyed whenever possible. Turnbridge tried to attack down the wings but first Paul Merchant and then Alex Anson defied them with critical tackles. After his tragic start to the game Paul was beginning to play with keenness and composure. He still preferred being up-front but for the present he was doing his best as a back-four player. One well-timed tackle that saved a dangerous situation brought warm congratulations from Alex, who'd decided he should do a bit of shouting, too, now he was vice-captain.

With their manager anxiously looking at his watch to see whether enough time remained for them to snatch the winner Turnbridge launched their last attack. From a mêlée just on the edge of the United box their centre-forward emerged with the ball. After jinking one way and then another to find an angle for a shot he lost patience with Alex's close marking and simply blasted the ball towards the net. It was going straight for Alex's face, and, instinctively, he flung up an arm to protect himself. The ball struck his wrist and bounced harmlessly away.

When the referee's whistle shrilled and the official pointed theatrically at the penalty-spot Damian couldn't believe what was happening.

'It can't be a penalty!' he protested. 'He didn't handle the ball. He just acted in self-defence, ref.'

The official frowned at him. 'Don't argue with me, son, unless you want your name in my little book. Now, remove yourself from the area before the kick is taken.'

Inevitably, it was the centre-forward himself who took the kick and, equally inevitably, he scored, in spite of Jonathan's dive along his line to reach the ball. A split-second after signalling the goal, the referee blew to end the match. Rovers 3, United 2.

The Darton players seemed stunned, and none more so than Alex. In an effort to console him as they trudged from the pitch, Damian put an arm round his shoulders.

'I'll tell you something,' he said, saying the first thing that came into his mind. 'The way things happen to us I reckon there must be a *diabolical* jinx on our team.'

Five

They sat in the Canary Café, the three of them, and wondered whether they should go. It had been Alex's idea but even he was beginning to have doubts about the venture. Damian supported him, because he felt anything that might help was worth trying. And Paul Merchant was willing to do whatever might be asked of him because he believed he was the cause of all the trouble in the first place. Paul's concentration on the discussion wasn't total, however, for he kept eyeing the rest of the chocolate fudge cake on the serving table by the counter.

'Probably he won't be in and then it'll be a wasted journey,' Alex said gloomily. 'Or if he is in he'll be too busy to see us without an appointment. The Secretary of the Football League is the sort of guy who'd only see *anybody* by appointment.'

'Mr Rayner is secretary of Redbourne Sunday League, not the *entire* Football League, and he works from home not in a colossal luxurious office in Lancashire,' Damian pointed out. 'And as it's eight o'clock at night he's not likely to have many people queuing up to see him. Honestly, it's worth a chance. He can only say no, forget it, if he doesn't like the idea – or if the rules won't allow it. He certainly won't bite our heads off just for asking. Right, Paul?'

Paul, at the mention of the word bite, had cast another longing glance at the rich cake and wasn't prepared for the question. Damian sighed with exasperation and nudged him back to reality.

'Quit thinking about feeding your face and concentrate on more important matters – if there is anything more important to you than stuffing yourself with cake,' Damian added with a touch of asperity. Somehow, Paul never seemed to do the right thing at the right time. 'I'm asking your opinion.'

'Oh yes,' said Paul, looking thoroughly guilty again. He really hadn't been listening properly. 'Look, I've told you what I think: I'm the one who's brought United all this bad luck. I broke Ian's leg and got Davey Scott sent off. So if you drop me for good the luck'll change. I'm ready to be sacrificed, you know.'

'Oh, stop wallowing in self-pity!' Damian responded. 'We can all do that very easily. We've already told you that things were bad before Ian got crocked. They've just got worse, that's all. We've got to do something *positive* to change our luck. We won't get anywhere if all we do is leave people out of the team. I'm ready this minute to go and see Mr

Rayner and tell him we want to change our name. It was Alex's idea but now he seems to be having second thoughts for some peculiar reason. So your vote is vital. Do we go or don't we?'

'We go,' replied Paul very promptly. He'd just made up his mind that he shouldn't have a third piece of cake after all: since buying a present for Ian, his money had almost run out.

'Right, that's two-to-one in favour, so let's not waste any more time.'

'No, it's three-nil,' declared Alex, draining the remainder of his pineapple juice and then getting to his feet. 'I was only being a bit cautious because I didn't want to talk you into something you were against. If this is a success I've got lots of other ideas we can work on, too.'

The proprietor of the Canary grinned at Paul as the boys edged past the counter on the way to the door. 'I'll keep the biggest piece of choc cake I can find for next time you're in,' he promised the young customer who returned with unfailing regularity. Paul was undeniably good for his business.

'Oh thanks – I'll try to look in tomorrow night,' replied Paul, distinctly cheering up again.

With Damian setting a pace that inhibited second thoughts, they walked briskly to the end terrace house that was the home of Richard Rayner. Carefully Damian mentally rehearsed his opening line for when Mr Rayner answered the door. He knew it was vital to give the right impression from the start. As it turned out, however, it was some moments before he was given a chance to say anything at all.

'Well, what a pleasure! A deputation of young gentlemen to see me,' was the instantaneous greeting from the tall, exceedingly thin and silver-haired secretary of the Sunday League. 'Please come right in and tell me what I can do to help you, gentlemen. I must say, you've chosen your moment well. I was just resting between labours, you see, so you've interrupted nothing of any consequence. Not at all, not at all.'

As they followed him down the passageway to a room at the back of the house the boys exchanged amused glances. Already they had the firm impression that Mr Rayner would never stop talking for anything. It also occurred to Alex that he hadn't even inquired whether it was him they wanted to see: but then, if he hadn't a wife or family any callers were bound to be seeking him. So perhaps he was lonely and glad of a chat with anyone and would be sympathetic to reasonable requests. Alex's hopes rose.

'Well, now, what can I offer you in the way of refreshments?' Mr Rayner inquired once they were all seated.

'Oh, I don't think we need anything to eat or drink, Mr Rayner,' Damian was starting to say when their host cut him off with a raised hand and ascending eyebrows.

'Nonsense, my dear young chap! Can't have people calling at my residence without offering them something, er, cheerful. Wouldn't do at all. How about a fizzy drink and a slice of plum cake?'

Paul's face immediately lit up at the prospect of something sweet to eat and it was really his response that sent Mr Rayner off to the kitchen with the promise that it wouldn't take a minute.

'Hey, he's very friendly, isn't he?' Paul said enthusiastically. 'He must really like us. Bet he'll agree to whatever we ask. I reckon this is the start of a whole new chapter for Darton United.'

Damian didn't say anything. He was still feeling somewhat overwhelmed by Mr Rayner's hospitable manner. There might, he feared, be a catch in it. On the other hand, perhaps the League secretary made a habit of welcoming every visitor with wide-open arms.

'Well now, you have my undivided attention,' said Mr Rayner quite formally after providing them with the refreshments and then settling in a high-backed leather armchair. 'But first, please tell me your names and the team you represent. If, as I have been assuming, you *do* represent a particular team in our League.'

Enthusiastically, Damian reeled off the intro-ductions and explained what he had in mind. 'You see, Mr Rayner, we believe that if we change our name we'll definitely change our luck. Anyway, United is a bit old fashioned, isn't it? I mean, if we called ourselves Sporting Darton – like Sporting Lisbon, you know, the team that does well in European matches – well, that'd be modern, really up-to-date. Or the other name is Dynamos – like Moscow and some other Russian outfit that I can't quite remember. Personally, I favour Darton Dynamos as the best choice but Alex and Paul here think it should be Sporting Darton. So do you think we could do it, then?'

Mr Rayner regarded him solemnly and silently for a few moments as if making up his mind exactly how to phrase his reply. Then, quite mildly, he inquired: 'Do you mean you wish to make a formal change so that in forthcoming fixtures your opponents will officially be playing Sporting Darton instead of Darton United?'

'That's right!' said Damian and Alex simultaneously.

'Out of the question, I'm afraid,' the secretary replied, to their considerable surprise. 'There is no provision in the rules of the Sunday League for any team to change its name in the middle of the season. Such a move would be bound to sow confusion and doubt all over the place. Your opponents wouldn't be at all sure whom they were playing if you turned up under a new guise. I'm sorry gentlemen, but your request cannot possibly be granted.'

Paul had suffered so many setbacks recently that he'd become almost used to them. He was beginning to learn how to face up to disappointments.

On this occasion, too, his enjoyment of the fruit cake helped to make him bolder than usual.

'Well, if we can't change our name, do you think we could change our shirts – I mean the colour of them?' he asked. 'You see, we think green is an unlucky colour – my dad says he never backs any horse with a jockey wearing green in *his* shirt colours. Dad says most racing people think that green brings back luck to the person wearing it.'

'Does your team have an official alternative strip?' Mr Rayner wanted to know.

'No chance!' said Damian with a half laugh. 'We can hardly afford one set of shirts between us. Any spare money we can get hold of is usually spent on travelling expenses. We're already saving like mad to buy another match ball for emergencies. We've only got one.'

'Oh dear.' Mr Rayner was now looking quite sad. 'I'm dreadfully sorry to have to turn you down again but the rules don't allow for colour changes in mid-season, either, except of course in dire emergency. And I hardly feel that your alleged bad luck qualifies as a dire emergency.'

'It does to us,' Damian muttered, half-hoping that Richard Rayner would choke on the orangeade he was now swallowing and so have to be replaced by a more sympathetic Sunday League secretary. 'If our luck gets any worse we'll have to pack up playing. I reckon that'll be an emergency.'

'A tragedy, Damian, a tragedy,' Mr Rayner corrected him with a wan smile. 'It is a tragedy when *any* team has to drop out of our League, whatever the reason. We must all strive to prevent that happening. But, I must tell you this: I invariably believe that when people talk about being dogged by bad luck they are simply failing to recognise their own shortcomings. They know a problem exists but they're not tackling it. They're trying to cover it up. And that won't do.'

'But what can we do?' Paul wanted to know. 'We've tried everything we can think of and nothing seems to work.'

'You've told me you've lost your manager. Well, have you thought of finding another one, somebody who has perhaps more expertise and would undertake to coach you in a more professional manner? Failing that, you could employ new tactics, a new approach to your playing skills. I'm quite sure that if you set about repairing the recent damage in a determined way then things will be bound to improve. But you have to *work* for success. When you meet an obstacle you have to find a way round it or over it. If you stick at something and do your best you'll come up with a solution eventually.'

He paused and then added: 'The fact that you've taken the trouble to come and see me tonight shows you have the right attitude. You've already proved to me that you're not the sort to surrender just because you're going through a bad patch. Gentlemen, I admire your spirit. But now. . . .'

Richard Rayner stood up and the boys followed suit. The meeting was over.

'Well, thanks very much for giving us so much of your time, Mr Rayner – oh, and for the cake and drinks,' said Damian.

'My pleasure. As I told you, I was just having a break when you arrived. But now I must get back to my twitching.'

They all stared at him, sure they must have misheard. But Alex couldn't resist asking for an explanation.

'Ah, you've not heard of the twitchers before?' said Mr Rayner, his eyebrows leaping high again above smiling eyes. 'Well, I suppose we are very rare birds, if I can put it that way. I always find that young people enjoy a good pun. Twitchers are bird watchers and twitching is our name for passing on vital information to one another about the location and the observation of unusual visitors to our shores. If we see something special we ring our pals so they can leap into their cars without delay and have a chance of a look for themselves. Before you came I was ringing round – and after you've gone I'll be contacting a few more friends. Monday is my favourite night of the week for this little task. Monday night is when most people seem to be at home, I find, so a bit of gossip is always welcome.'

Only Alex knew what to say in answer to that unexpected revelation. 'Actually, Mr Rayner, I'm a bird watcher myself. I'm often up on the cliffs studying seabirds. Have you, er, ever seen any really fantastic bird? You know, that hardly ever is seen in Britain?'

He nodded with remembered satisfaction. 'Indeed, yes. I was once exceedingly fortunate to get a call from a friend in Yorkshire who had just identified a desert wheatear. I was able to dash there and get a glimpse for myself. Really, it shouldn't have been anywhere near our country. It should then have been in North Africa. But we decided it must have become disorientated – lost its sense of direction, I mean, and flown north instead of south. That sort of thing can happen with birds. And with humans too, I shouldn't wonder. Still, I musn't delay you all with my ramblings. You'll be wanting to get back to your homes. So – '

Alex, however, had decided that a final appeal might still stand a chance of being successful.

'Mr Rayner, as we both have the same hobby,' he began tentatively, 'do you think you could do us a great favour and change your mind? I mean, let us change our name so that we can change our luck? Please.'

His fellow players turned back and looked expectantly at the tall figure of the League secretary. But now, with an air of some sadness, he was shaking his head.

'I'm afraid that would be quite improper. I really

couldn't make an exception, not even for a fellow ornithologist.'

'No, of course not,' Alex agreed. 'We do understand. Goodnight, Mr Rayner.'

Six

Ian Venn was demonstrating how adept he was at getting around even without the usual support of a crutch or walking stick. His main difficulty at first, he said, had been in keeping his balance because of the extra weight on one side of his body. But, he added in typical fashion, he'd quickly taught himself how to cope with that situation.

When, at last, he sat down and put his leg up on a footstool his visitors admitted they were impressed by his progress. None of them had ever broken a leg and so they hadn't been sure what to expect when calling on the boy who so briefly had been captain of their team. Paul had even suggested that Ian might be too drowsy to talk to them because he'd been under the influence of pain-killing drugs.

'So you don't get any trouble with it, then?' asked Damian.

'Well, not much. Some sharp twinges of pain now and again – bones knitting together again, I imagine. But everybody says the plaster makes you itch like mad after a time. And, of course, you can't have a jolly good scratch when you want to under there! Hey, I think it's time you guys put your autographs on my plaster – if you can find a space!'

Ian himself offered a pen and they lined up to sign.

'Got anybody famous among this lot?' Paul inquired.

'Not since I started the whole thing off with my own signature,' Ian laughed.

'It'd be great if you could get some famous First Division players to drop in and sign up for you,' said Alex. 'You often see pictures in the papers of top stars signing the plaster casts of other players in hospitals or clinics or wherever they finish up. Then, when they're removed, the casts are auctioned for charity, aren't they? If we did that, we could raise some cash for United.'

'Hey, that's not a bad idea, not bad at all,' Ian enthused, and the others nodded their agreement. 'But first, tell me about the visit to Mr Rayner's. I realise it didn't work out. If it had, you'd've been bursting to give me all the details as soon as you got here.'

That couldn't be denied. Damian explained how hospitable the League secretary had been but that he couldn't amend the rules for the sake of United.

'We all liked him but, frankly, he wasn't much help,' he concluded. 'The only thing he could sug-

gest was that we found ourselves another manager
or a coach. Somebody with expertise – a professional, really.'

'A professional *footballer*, did he mean?' Ian
asked immediately. 'Hey, that's good thinking, too.
Maybe that's what we should do right away. It'd
give the rest of the players a great boost, wouldn't
it?'

'What, you mean to come and sign your plaster
cast so that it'll be worth a lot more money
when – '

'No, you idiot, Paul!' Ian rolled his eyes heaven-
wards. 'Forget the plaster. We're talking about
68

getting a *coach* – a top player who would turn us into a better team. Come to think of it, that shouldn't be hard for anybody!'

'No *professional* would give up his spare time to looking after us,' Alex declared. 'I mean, they only want to be involved with successful teams.'

'Not necessarily,' replied Damian with the air of one who was thinking things through. 'Lots of League teams have boys of our age as mascots. Well, this would be the situation in reverse. A good player would be bound to think that he could do something for us because we *are* at the bottom. He'd get a kick out of lifting us up – and he'd be sure to do that, all right. If we were right at the top then he might reckon he'd only be jumping on the bandwagon – or that a top team didn't need him. No, I believe it's got a good chance of working.'

'Exactly!' said Ian, warming to the idea which had come to him almost by accident. 'If we go the right way about asking for help – you know, not ask too much – then I'm sure we'll succeed. But we've got to be enthusiastic in our approach. I was reading yesterday – I get a lot of time for reading at present – that enthusiasm is catching, like measles! It always rubs off on people.'

'You can't rub measles spots off, though, can you?' Alex remarked drily. He knew he had to say something funny to recover lost ground.

They discussed whom they should choose. Because of the travelling that would be involved, they had to go for someone who lived in the area. Redbourne City were the local Second Division club, and, by common consent, Bryn Marsden was the star player. Earlier in his career he'd played for Liverpool and then West Ham United but, according to newspaper critics, it was only in the last couple of seasons that his skills had really blossomed. He was the inspiration behind City's recent surge up the table and, what's more, he'd scored in six successive games.

Bryn Marsden was the unanimous choice of the newly- (and self-) elected Management Committee of Darton United F.C. to be their coach and honorary President. He was to be informed immediately by letter.

'But how do we start it off?' Ian wanted to know. 'I mean if we call him "Dear Bryn" he might think we were being a bit cheeky because we don't know him personally. Well not yet, anyway. But "Dear Mr Marsden" sounds too – what's the word? – oh, formal. He might think it's just a begging letter for extra money. My dad always chucks those sort of letters into the bin without even reading them all through. We don't want Bryn Marsden doing that.'

They debated that point and the rest of the contents during the next half-hour. Six drafts were made before they settled on the final version of the letter. Paul, who had his own typewriter, offered to type the original and four copies but that was turned down because the consensus of opinion was that a handwritten letter had more personal appeal. They used Ian's address and enclosed a list of United's fixtures. The letter read:

Dear Bryn Marsden,

We, the undersigned members of Darton United F.C., would like you to be our official coach and honorary President. We play in the Sunday League every Sunday afternoon. We have to confess that we're not a very good team. Actually, we're pretty dreadful because we're bottom of our section. But we are very determined and are keen to do our best at all times. We think that if you came to coach us we would improve terrifically.

We are all keen fans of Redbourne City F.C. and go to matches whenever we can. You, of course, are our favourite player and always have been. So we are really looking forward to seeing you at our next match – or when you can make it. We know we'll start improving after that.

We send you all our best wishes and hope you score a hat-trick on Saturday.

Yours sincerely,
(*Signed*) Damian Tennant, Alexander Anson, Paul Merchant and Ian Venn

PS   The address above is Ian Venn's. He's broken a leg and so can't play for a few weeks. Damian is the team captain.

They all read it through several times to see whether it contained any faults and whether it could be improved upon. Alex, who claimed that English was his best subject at school, pointed out that the word 'keen' had been used twice; but Ian said that 'keen' really summed up their attitude as committee and so there was nothing wrong in repeating that word. Damian and Paul agreed with that view and so Alex withdrew his objection. Because, by common consent, his handwriting was the neatest and clearest Alex wrote the final copy that was to be posted. Ian, meanwhile, hobbled off to persuade his mother to part with a first-class postage stamp.

'Well, all we can do now is keep our fingers crossed that he'll turn up at our next match,' remarked Alex as the letter and fixture list were sealed into the envelope which was then addressed to Bryn Marsden at City's football ground. As an afterthought Alex added 'Urgent' in the top left-hand corner.

'If he looks at the Sunday League tables in the *Echo* and sees how rotten our playing record really is, he probably won't come within ten miles of us,' Damian said in a moment of pessimism.

'We'll just have to risk that,' was Ian's philosophical reply. 'But even if he doesn't come to help us we'll at least have done *something* to try and change our bad luck. We're not lying down and letting disaster roll right over us. We'll be proving

72

to everybody that we're not giving in, whatever happens. Right?'

'Right!' was the firm and unanimous reply.

Seven

With a flick of his wrists Damian tipped another shovelful of snow over the touchline and then took a long look at the sky. It was the colour, he decided, of a lump of old plasticine, and just about as cheerful. If there wasn't a lot more snow up there he'd be amazed. Even if only a little of it fell during the next hour or so, United's away match with Eppleby Village Colts would surely have to be abandoned. On reflection, though, that might not be the worst thing that had ever happened to United.

On arrival at the ground, which was actually part of the attractive village green beside a railed duck pond, Damian had been informed by the home team's skipper that Billy Sandford wouldn't be turning up. Mr Sandford had telephoned to say that his son couldn't play because he was suffering from tonsillitis. Damian wondered how true that was. It could be that Billy was sulking because he was no longer captain; or that his father simply preferred to sever all family connections with the team he formerly managed. Still, at least Mr Sandford had let them know what was happening. Nowadays the Darton players made their own way to matches and so until they all assembled the captain had no way of knowing, in advance of the kick-off, who'd be present. As it was, they'd now have only the minimum number. Davey Scott, who'd served his period of suspension for attacking Paul Merchant, would have to be promoted from substitute to makeshift striker. So it was to be hoped that they all avoided injury during the game.

In spite of the Arctic weather of that weekend, the pitch, under its covering of snow, was not nearly so hard as the players supposed. The groundsman, who was intensely proud of his handiwork, wasn't too pleased when the referee insisted that some at least of the snow should be removed before the game began so that the touchlines and other markings could be seen clearly by the officials. Reluctantly, he'd handed out shovels and brushes to every boy within reach and then stalked from one group of workers to another to make sure none of them damaged his precious turf. More than once he could be heard trying to persuade the referee to postpone the fixture because 'there's a cartload of snow up there still and half of it's sure to come down before this game's over. Best to take sensible precautions now.' The ref, however, had been abroad for a couple of weeks on a business trip and was keen to get back into action again.

Eppleby were equally anxious to play. They were having a run of success and could see a chance of snatching promotion after an indifferent start to the season. Their star player was their skipper and top goal-scorer, Gareth Green, who had played several games for Redbourne City Boys' team and was soon to have a trial for the county. The Colts – or the VC's as their supporters preferred to call them – had every reason to believe that they'd easily de-molish Darton United, still without so much as a single League point. True, United had also shown some recent improvement but not enough to achieve a draw let alone a victory. There'd been no

response at all to the letter to Bryn Marsden and even Damian was beginning to feel a little depressed by the lack of success. He couldn't see what more he could do to lift the team. Only victory would do that now, he supposed.

Light flakes of snow were swirling across the pitch when, at last, the match began. As Damian had anticipated, Eppleby had a strong tendency to play every ball they could to Gareth Green. That didn't particularly help their cause because even Gareth at his best couldn't outwit a posse of hard-tackling defenders. Usually he tried to as if he had perpetually to prove to himself how many skills he possessed. In training sessions, United had concentrated on tackling quickly and forcefully. For the first time, it began to look as if all that hard work was paying off. Damian had nominated himself and Paul Merchant as the first line of defence against Gareth's wiles and, by good fortune, both had got their timing right in the early stages of the match. Gareth began to collect a few bruises for he scorned the use of shinpads. Several times the ref blew up for fouls on the star striker but none of them was severe enough to merit a caution. Then, when he did escape the attentions of Damian and Paul, Gareth found that Alex Anson was just as tough a proposition. Inevitably, Gareth had to start laying the ball off if his team was going to succeed.

When Eppleby at last broke through and had a clear sight of goal they discovered that Jonathan

McGuigan was in superlative form. He'd been improving rapidly ever since taking over from Davey Scott and now he excelled himself. Within a minute he'd fingertipped round the post a searing shot from Gareth's co-striker; and then, with a startling reflex save, blocked a piledriver from Gareth himself at point-blank range.

'Terrific, Jonathan, terrific!' Damian sang out as he hurried to take up a defensive position for the resultant corner kick. He couldn't remember seeing a better save than that one.

Even the Colts' supporters vigorously applauded the goalkeeper's performance. 'Well, of course, he must have had plenty of practice considering the state of their defence – it's always been like a sieve,' remarked one man, unaware of the fact that Jonathan was a relative newcomer to the side.

There wasn't much doubt, in Damian's view, that Jonathan was proving to be an inspiration to the rest of United's defence. Their growing confidence in his ability to keep the opposition at bay was now extending to their own play. Determination to succeed was replacing desperation: their first instinct was no longer to clear the ball from their penalty area at all costs. They had started to pass the ball to a team-mate decisively and accurately. Panic was in the past.

Unhappily, there wasn't any sign of improvement up front. Neil Dallimore was as clumsy as ever and though Stevie Pailthorp was still prepared to run hard and fast he wasn't getting anywhere. Discouragingly, it was already beginning to look as if Davey Scott was a better goalkeeper than a forward! So far he hadn't even managed to trap or kick the ball properly when it reached him. At present, United's attack was no better than a joke. Damian wondered whether he dare switch roles in the second half with Neil. If Neil could be persuaded to mark Gareth Green, sticking to him like superglue, then his height and unpredictable awkwardness just might put the Eppleby skipper out of his stride. The whole ploy was a risk – but perhaps one worth taking if it enabled United to set up some attacking moves.

Damian decided to postpone any decision until the interval. He might even ask Neil what he thought of the idea, though he could guess the striker's reaction. Dallimore believed that only sheer bad luck prevented him from being one of the League's most prolific goal-scorers but that one day his real talent would be recognised.

Every gesture of the referee's was flamboyant and he brought the first half to an end with vigorous scissors movements of his arms following a piercing blast on his whistle. United had the greater cause for satisfaction: after all, they had not conceded a goal in spite of all the pressure they'd been under right from the kick-off. For their part, Eppleby felt they had the measure of their opponents. It was surely only a question of time before they got the ball in the net. Gareth Green would break out of his personal stranglehold in the second half. That was what his manager told him, anyway.

'Look, we've done terrifically so far – especially the defence,' Damian said as his players gathered around him. A few had brought their own refreshments but by now the spirit of the side was such that they offered to share them with those who had nothing. 'But we mustn't relax in the second half. We've all got to concentrate, really *concentrate*, just as much as ever. If things go our way then we can hit Eppleby on the break and win our first match. I really mean that.'

It was a matter of great satisfaction to Damian that not one member of the team looked as though he doubted that statement. Then he explained the tactical change he had in mind if United didn't manage to score within ten minutes of the start of the second half. This time Neil himself had some reservations about the plan, just as Damian had anticipated.

'Yes, I realise you feel you're wasting your talents just marking somebody out of the game,' Damian told the gangling striker calmly. 'But a good player should be able to play *anywhere* in the team. The main thing is, though, this move is for the benefit of the whole side. That's what counts most. O.K.?'

Even Neil found it impossible to argue against that view and so, albeit sulkily, he agreed to do his best. Predictably, Eppleby resumed like the weather: driving forward relentlessly in fierce gusts. Once again, however, Darton's defence held firm. Of course, by now they were becoming specialists in rearguard actions. Then, just when it seemed that they might be getting the upper hand, things went dreadfully wrong.

Damian had made his switch with Neil and twice had sent Stevie Pailthorp on challenging runs to the edge of the Eppleby box. Davey Scott was trying to make his own impression on the opposition when, quite savagely, he was cut down by a wild tackle. Anticipating the award of a free kick Damian darted forward to grab the ball – and was knocked to the ground by a blow from the referee's hand that caught him across the throat. The official, who hadn't seen Damian's approach from behind, had simply been demonstrating in his customary dramatic style, his disapproval of the Eppleby player's tackle before awarding a free kick.

The pain was terrible. Damian was sure he was going to be sick – and yet he was also gasping for breath as he writhed on the ground. The whole thing had happened so suddenly he didn't even know what had struck him.

'Son, I'm sorry, truly sorry!' the referee was saying over and over again as he knelt on the turf and tried to cradle Damian's head in his arms. Already Eppleby's manager was rushing on to the pitch with the medical bag. He had seen the entire incident and was aware of how serious the injury could be.

'How does it feel now?' the two men asked but, for the present, Damian was quite unable to answer. The pain was receding a little but he still felt as if he were dying. His throat was on fire.

Someone was offering him a drink. Although he heard a voice inquiring 'Is it wise to allow him to drink?' he swallowed some of the orange juice. He needed it. For a moment he thought he was going to bring it straight back but, luckily, it stayed down. Marginally, his throat felt easier; but he still didn't dare try to speak.

'Look, let's get him to the touch-line – and for goodness' sake put a coat or a rug over him,' the Eppleby manager was saying.

A woman spectator also came forward to help. She claimed to have nursing experience and carried out a gentle but thorough inspection of Damian's mouth and jaw and neck. Gradually he began to feel better although his throat felt very sore.

'I don't think anything's damaged,' the young woman told him comfortingly. 'Just take things easy and you should soon be perfectly all right again. You've been very lucky it wasn't worse. It looked awful when it happened. But it was a pure accident. The referee just didn't see you coming up behind him. He's a bit of an extrovert, isn't he? Should be on the stage!'

'Lucky' wasn't a word Damian would have used. His team was down to ten men – and, as he began to focus on the game again, they also went a goal down. Gareth evaded another of Neil Dallimore's unco-ordinated tackles, sprinted into the penalty area, cleverly slipped the ball past Paul Merchant, rounded the defender on the other side and then crashed an unstoppable shot past Jonathan's right shoulder. His team-mates greeted him like the hero he was. With time running out they'd feared Eppleby were going to be held to a humiliating draw.

Damian started to get to his feet to rejoin his team; now they needed him more than ever if United were to salvage anything from the match. His temporary nurse, however, restrained him.

'I think you'd be better off resting because you still look very pale,' she told him. 'It's getting near the end, anyway. And, after all, it's only a game! Your health comes first, young man!'

He would have gritted his teeth at that remark if only his mouth wasn't so sore. It was true that he was still feeling a bit groggy. On the other hand, a captain should be prepared to overcome the pain barrier for the sake of his team.

'You know, it's really bad luck on Darton to lose a goal just when their best player's been carried off after a karate chop from the referee!' remarked one of the men on the touchline within Damian's hearing. His friend laughed and said that 'karate chop' just about described the blow. Damian was marginally comforted by knowing that someone, at least, considered him to be United's star player. But that would count for nothing if they didn't score a goal in the remaining few minutes. He felt he should be urging his side on but he didn't want to risk further damage to his throat.

Alex had automatically assumed the leadership but he was being kept busy trying to subdue the revitalised Eppleby forwards. What they'd done once they felt they could do again: and it was plain that another goal would clinch the match for them. Gareth was seeing plenty of the ball again and, inevitably, making good use of his opportunities. Dallimore was totally bemused by his opponent's skills and against them could offer only brute force.

After bringing Gareth crashing to the ground on the edge of the penalty area, Neil received a severe warning as well as a booking and Eppleby had a free kick from a dangerous range. Damian desperately wanted to be on the pitch to organise the defence. He sensed that this time Gareth, ruefully rubbing a bruised knee, would act as a decoy. Pulling away from his medical adviser, Damian darted down the touchline to attract Alex's attention.

At that moment Alex, looking towards Damian, caught sight of someone else approaching the playing area from the path by the duck-pond.

'Hey!' he cried excitedly. 'Bryn Marsden's here! He's come to see us at last.'

Simultaneously the referee signalled for the kick to be taken. The ball was floated perfectly for the tallest Eppleby midfielder to head it back across the box to where Gareth, oblivious of the ache in his knee, could collect it and, in the same fluid movement, drive the ball through the gap between the stationary Jonathan and the far upright. It was one of the simplest goals Gareth Green had scored for several matches.

Of course, the whole thing had been made a good deal easier for him by the attitude of the Darton defenders. Most of them had been completely distracted by Alex's dramatic announcement. Beside the arrival of the man they believed was going to be their official coach and honorary President, everything else was fairly insignificant. Even Damian, as elated as anyone by the appearance of the Redbourne City star, missed seeing Gareth Green's goal. When it dawned on him what had happened he covered his dismay by going forward to introduce himself to the familiar tall, slightly stooping figure of his favourite player.

'Good to meet you, Damian.' The words were as warm as the handshake. 'Sorry it took me so long to get round to it. But we've just moved house and every spare minute away from playing and training seems to have been taken up with sticking tiles on walls or painting anything that stands still for five minutes on the trot! Anyway, I seem to have chosen a bad moment to turn up. Sorry about that. Better fill me in on what's been happening overall.'

Within two minutes it seemed to Damian that he and Bryn Marsden had been friends for years. He was amazed how easy it was to talk to him. Bryn, however, appeared to be genuinely interested in the progress (or lack of it) of Darton United and concerned about Damian's own mishap with the referee. Then, when the final whistle blew, he made a point of applauding the United players from the field and sympathising with them in their defeat. Players from both sides crowded round for autographs as soon as they could lay their hands on anything that could be signed; patiently he signed for every one of them. Eventually, however, the Eppleby Village Colts and their supporters departed. By now, the snow had stopped falling and, as far as Damian and his fellow committee members were concerned, the day had begun to improve enormously.

'Are you going to accept our invitation to be our coach and President?' asked Damian anxiously, voicing the question that was in all their minds.

'Sure I am!' was the enthusiastic response. 'Do you know, I get all sorts of invitations from all sorts of people but nobody's ever asked me to be President of their football team. I think it's terrific and I'm really flattered, boys. When I played in a schoolboy side we had a marvellous chap helping us. So if I can give you something of what he gave us I'll feel I'm really putting something back into the game.'

'But you know we're not a very good team, don't you?' said Alex. 'I mean we've just lost again this afternoon and we must be hot favourites to be

relegated at the end of the season. Sympathy alone is not going to be enough, is it?'

'You've hit the nail right on the head, son! We've got to be practical and find positive ways of improving in all departments of the team. O.K., you're on the deck now but you've got spirit and you're keen – you told me that in your letter and I believe you. Well, we'll build on that for a start. We'll get down to some really organised training with he aim of developing individual skills *and* teamwork. How about that?'

They nodded, eagerly.

'I can get the use of a sports hall for a couple of

hours on Monday nights,' Bryn continued. 'I think that's the ideal time because we can analyse what happened on Sunday and then plan the improvements for the week ahead. If you can make it then, I think we should start as soon as possible. Which means tomorrow night. O.K.?'

'O.K.!' they chorused.

Eight

'Are you absolutely *sure* you're feeling all right?' Damian's mother asked him anxiously as he swallowed a piece of apple with, apparently, some difficulty. 'If your throat's still bothering you I'd rather you went to see the doctor instead of traipsing off to *another* football meeting. Now tell me the truth.'

'No, it's fine now, honestly,' Damian tried to assure her. 'I mean, I just bit off a bit more than I could chew – if you see what I mean. Shouldn't have swallowed it all in one go. Anyway, it's not just a *meeting*. We're going to be coached at the Sports Centre by Bryn Marsden himself. I can't miss that – nobody can. Even Ian's going to be there and he's still got a broken leg. Look, I told you, Mum: the throat's only a bit sore if I swallow a lot at once. Otherwise it's improving all the time.'

Mrs Tennant gave him a dubious look but let the subject drop. Normally she allowed him to judge his own fitness for football but the knock on the neck worried her. Damian himself would never have mentioned it but Alex had rashly referred to the incident in Mrs Tennant's hearing during a visit to the house the previous evening. Since then Damian had been obliged to give his mother regular reports on the state of his health. He just wished she would believe him when he said that he was feeling perfectly fit again.

Deliberately he took a long swig of milk, making sure that she noticed; normally he liked milk no better than yogurt but it was supposed to be a body food. Moreover, he'd improved it first by adding soda water from a siphon.

'Right then, I'm off,' he announced with great cheerfulness. 'Shan't be late because Ian's dad has promised to bring me back in their car. Oh yes – and I finished my homework before tea. Bye then.'

At the Sports Centre on the edge of town they didn't have to wait for Bryn Marsden to turn up; he'd arrived ahead of any of them. What impressed them still more was that he was wearing his official Redbourne City strip of scarlet shirt and shorts with white-banded black socks and training shoes.

'Proves you've got guts if you turn up for training when you've got a broken leg,' he remarked with grin as he shook hands with Ian Venn. 'No trainer can ask for more than that. Right then, boys, gather round and I'll tell you what the master plan is for tonight.'

He explained that they were going to begin from

the beginning with the most fundamental part of the game of soccer: passing. Everything was built on that and therefore if a player couldn't pass the ball properly he was no good at all to any team. Even the goalie had to learn that skill because, if injured, he might have to become an outfield player. In the few minutes he'd been present at Sunday's game, Bryn went on, he'd seen some examples of poor passing, particularly with the toe-end. That had to be banished, for a start. The ball should be passed with the inside or outside of the foot. Accurate passing had to be achieved as soon as possible but there was no point in moving on to other skills until it had been mastered.

'So,' he concluded, 'the first part of this session may become a bit boring for you. But we've got to work at it until we get it right. And when we do get it right you'll already have become much better players. *Much* better.'

Twelve players had turned up, including Billy Sandford, who sheepishly explained to Ian and Damian that it hadn't been his wish to miss the match against Eppleby; and yes, his tonsillitis seemed to have cleared up by itself with remarkable speed. Bryn Marsden split them up into pairs and then had them form parallel lines a dozen or so metres apart. The object was to keep each ball in motion with the partners passing to each other, first using the favoured foot, then switching to the weaker foot.

On the unyielding artificial surface of the sports hall it wasn't easy to judge the bounce of what appeared to be a fairly light ball and so initially the passing was pretty ragged. One or two of the players soon started to joke about their incompetence when a pass was badly misdirected or someone stumbled over the ball. Bryn, however, instantly clamped down on what he described as 'a totally unprofessional attitude'. He added: 'the only time to laugh is when you've beaten the opposition hollow in a Cup Final or a top-of-the-League clash. And you haven't done that yet.'

He moved easily from pair to pair, from time to time demonstrating how to apply the right technique, and gradually a rhythm built up. Then, just as they had got used to their partnerships, the pairings were switched. Damian, who'd been linked with Alex Anson, now found himself having to combine with Davey Scott. Passing had long been one of Damian's specialities and he'd even begun to feel a bit superior about his accomplishment in this company. Working with Davey quickly helped to change that outlook.

'Oh, come on, Scottie, you can do better than that!' Damian called in exasperation after retrieving the ball from the back of the hall following another wild kick from his companion.

'Look, you're not the teacher,' Davey snapped back. 'Just because you're captain – *temporary* captain – doesn't give you the right to – '

'Hey, simmer down, simmer down!' Bryn Marsden interrupted. 'We're not going to get anywhere as a team if you're at each other's throats *in training*. Discipline in a team is very important and Damian *is* the captain, Davey. He's simply wanting to get the best out of everybody for the team's sake. Well, now I think it's time we had a break. You've all been working pretty hard so you deserve a rest. Now, who'll volunteer to fetch us all some drinks from the cafeteria? Oh, and before anyone starts to argue, I'm paying for the first round because I'm your President!'

While they all sipped coffee and Cokes and fruit

juices he talked to them about team morale and tactical matters. It was easy to forget, he pointed out, that soccer was a team game because spectators and commentators were always referring to the skills and performances of individuals. 'But a team will only be successful if they play as a team. That's true at whatever level you play, from your Sunday League to international matches. However brilliant, one player can't win games on his own. I saw last Sunday that too many times you played, many of you, without much thought for your team-mates. Not passing when *they* wanted the ball, not looking up to see who was being marked before giving the ball to a team-mate. Once we all start thinking alike, thinking about *our* team, then we'll be making great progress, I promise you. As I've seen tonight, most of you have skills as well as an aptitude for learning how to improve. We're going to build on all that, week by week.'

They found him very easy to get on with and, gradually, they stopped thinking of him as simply a star player they were lucky to have met in person. They began to accept him as their coach or manager: the man who would guide them to success. When they made a mistake or said something foolish, he told them so. Praise was something he gave only when it was earned.

In the second half of the evening he stepped up the tempo. The players formed groups and had to pass the ball while on the move and then when challenged by opponents. In the final minutes Bryn himself joined in and interest soared as individuals made supreme efforts to deliver the perfect pass to him. But he turned down a plea that there should be a six-a-side game, involving everyone, as a finale.

'I've had a long day,' he said with a grin, 'and I'm sure you have, too. Look, I want you to enjoy these sessions and you won't enjoy them if you finish them feeling totally exhausted. At City we always like to keep a bit in reserve and I think you should do the same. O.K.?'

'Will you be coming to all our Sunday League matches, Bryn?' Paul Merchant wanted to know.

'I can't promise that, son. I've got a family of my own, you know, as well as a new house to work on. I'll turn up when I can because, naturally, I want to see how the coaching sessions are going to help you when the chips are down. But there are going to be times when I just can't make it for one reason or another. But I promise you this: only an absolute emergency will keep me away from these Monday night training spots. And if I am unable to get here, well, I'll do all in my power to get a team-mate from Redbourne City to stand in for me. And he'll be given a copy of the programme I've worked out for you.'

'What will we be doing next week, then?' Billy inquired a split-second before Damian could ask the identical question.

'Ah, that's what I like – keenness! If you're already looking forward to the next session things must be good. Well, first of all we'll see how much you've remembered about passing the ball. So after we've revised that I hope to move on to controlling the ball – trapping it, checking it, not just with the foot but with the body, on the chest, in the tummy and on the thigh. Very useful skills at all times.'

Bryn paused but they were all gazing at him so expectantly that he decided to summarize the rest of the training programme he had drawn up. Tactics, he explained, might come next, knowing when to run both with the ball and off the ball, when to tackle and when to stand off; and so on. Another session would be devoted to heading, a skill which few boys mastered at an early age. Then it would be time to specialise in tackling and dribbling.

'If you absorb all that lot then you'll be on the road to success,' he concluded. 'So, when the crunch comes, the entire *team* will be properly equipped to cope with it. O.K.?'

By now they were all used to his style.

'O.K.!' they agreed.

Then he added: 'But just remember this: you've still got to work on the things you've learned. They won't stay with you unless you keep polishing them. As one of my old bosses used to say, if you look after your talents properly they'll look after you when you need 'em most – when that crunch comes.'

Nine

The 'crunch' that Bryn Marsden mentioned turned out to be the game against Tinacre Rangers. It could not have been more vital. For the team that lost would be relegated.

In the weeks since the Redbourne City star had taken over as their coach and President, Darton United really had blended skills with endeavour. After picking up points with successive draws they'd achieved their first win of the season. True, the opposition had not been formidable. French Hill Eagles were the team directly above them in the League: but Darton triumphed 5–3 after being a goal down at the interval. That success was another inspiration for the following Sunday they won again, this time overcoming a team in the top half of the table with the help of a penalty awarded in the last minute of the game. Damian had taken that responsibility upon himself and, with a coolness he was still proud of, had slotted the ball into the net by the left-hand upright for the winning goal. Bryn had been present at that match and later rewarded Damian with the gift of a City shirt 'for playing a captain's part to the full'.

As the season reached its climax they clawed their way over French Hill and so lifted themselves from the bottom of the table for the first time in their history. Now, with just one match remaining, they were level on points with Tinacre Rangers. To some, it seemed as if fate had intervened to arrange the most dramatic fixture possible. For United's final match at home was against Tinacre – and Rangers' goal difference was superior to United's. So United *had* to win to survive.

While Tinacre had been having a very bad run of results – losing each of their previous six games – United had been in good form. The time they'd devoted to training and building up their skills under Bryn's direction had plainly been well spent. Practically every member of the squad had become a fitness fanatic and Paul, for instance, was able to announce proudly that he'd completely given up eating cake at any time. Ian Venn had made remarkable progress in recovering from his broken leg: he'd started light training again and declared that, in an emergency, he'd even be prepared to turn out in the Tinacre match.

Damian had pondered whether to choose Ian as substitute but in the end decided against it. The risks, for both player and team, were too great. But it would be good to have Ian on the touchline, giving the team all the encouragement he could, especially as Bryn couldn't be present until half-time at the earliest. Their inspirational coach had promised to attend a friend's birthday lunch party in a neighbouring village and had confessed to the boys that it might well be difficult for him to get back in time for the second half. In his absence, Damian and Ian would have to cope with the pre-match pep talk. The United players no longer needed to be motivated: they knew exactly what was required of them by now and how they should set about achieving it. On the other hand, there'd been ominous signs in the last two matches that several were being affected by nerves as tension built up. Some of the old elementary mistakes had occurred again; and more than once defenders had panicked under pressure. Both games had been won by a single goal after United had held a useful lead.

Against Tinacre Rangers, who would be just as desperate to win, any nervous error at all might prove fatal. And then United's gallant struggle against relegation would be lost.

It was Bryn Marsden's belief, which he had drilled into the United players, that a team should concern itself with building up its own strengths and ambitions and not waste time worrying about the quality and the plans of the opposition. All the same, Damian felt he couldn't ignore the menace of Rangers' best player, a tall, strongly-built mid-fielder called Lee Shoscombe, famous for his surging runs on goal from deep positions. Damian was reminded of the problem of trying to curb Eppleby's star player, Gareth Green: they'd kept him quiet for most of the time but, in the end, he'd won the match for his side. Since then, however, United's defence had improved greatly and so there'd be no need to use a striker, Neil Dallimore, to try and mark an opponent out of the game. Neil had actually learned quite a lot from Bryn Marsden and was now playing the best football of his life. What's more, he was also United's leading scorer.

No, Damian resolved at last, they wouldn't try to anticipate what Rangers might do: they'd simply play in their own style and hope to be at their best. And keep their fingers crossed that luck would be on their side, too.

'Right, then,' Damian told his team-mates as they were all about to leave the dressing-room, 'we know we're a better team than Tinacre. So let's just go out there and prove it.'

He licked his lips, hoped he'd concealed his own nervousness, and led his team out on to the pitch at a very fast pace. Deliberately he'd waited for Rangers to take the field first. Now they would see United coming at them, looking as determined and unstoppable as a fleet of green-and-yellow excavators. To add to the effect, United were greeted by prolonged applause from the biggest crowd ever to support them.

Damian, however, would thankfully have swopped at least half of those spectators for the presence of Bryn Marsden. On the other hand, if United could win without his guidance then it would surely prove that they really had matured as a team. Their success would truly be deserved.

Rangers, all in red, didn't give the impression they were riddled with anxieties. After winning the toss, they chose to defend with the sun in their eyes and calmly allowed United to launch the first attack of the game. When the ball ran clear to one of their deep-lying midfielders he didn't simply boot it up-field. Almost nonchalantly he took it round one United player, then another, before sending a splendidly-judged pass to one of his strikers. Such coolness drew appreciative applause even from United fans.

It occurred then to Damian that Tinacre, because of their recent bad results and the fact that they were playing away to desperate rivals, had resigned themselves to defeat. They would simply try their best and hope not to suffer too severely, which meant that they could play in a very relaxed manner. That could only make things harder still for Darton.

At the earliest opportunity Damian set up another attack and supplied Stevie Pailthorp with the chance to run at, and unsettle, Rangers' defence. Stevie's speed was still his chief asset, though now he'd learned to use it in bursts. Very sensibly, he kept to the touchline to draw the full-backs apart and then sent over a good-looking centre. Unfortunately, Neil's timing was not as good as his jump and the ball passed over his head as Neil was coming down to earth again. Still, the United fans had seen something to shout about for their own team and the cheers were further encouragement to Stevie.

For the next few minutes there was too much aimless play with neither side able to build up a movement worthy of the name. The first goal was probably going to be vital and each defence was absolutely determined not to be the one to concede it. Those in the middle of the field tended to push the ball around among themselves and almost inevitably it went to a player already heavily marked. So there was no progress in any direction. Of course, it would satisfy Tinacre to hold out for a draw and so they didn't need to exert themselves.

'Come on, let's get a grip on this game!' Damian yelled fiercely as Davey Scott gave away a free kick with a clumsy foul on a Tinacre striker. The offence occurred only just inside the United half but the ball was hammered right into the heart of the penalty area. Unnoticed by all the United players, Lee Shoscombe came through at panther-like speed to meet the ball and head for goal.

Jonathan McGuigan, who'd hesitated about whether to come out, just managed to get a finger-tip to the ball – and that was enough to deflect it on to, and then over, the bar. United had given away a corner. But it had so very nearly been a goal.

Shoscombe himself, who plainly had his own fan club behind the goal, jostled with Jonathan for a prime position on the goal-line as the corner was about to be taken. Damian was deeply worried about the threat from the tall Rangers midfielder. He'd been furious that he hadn't spotted Lee's diagonal run into the box. Lee wasn't the sort of boy to miss twice from that range.

Fortunately, the kick was short and Alex Anson had no difficulty in heading the ball away from the danger zone. Then the ball was pushed across to Paul Merchant as the Tinacre players streamed back upfield in expectation of a counter-attack from United's forwards.

Afterwards, Paul wasn't able to give a convincing explanation of what he'd really been trying to do when he caused the disaster. As he faced his own goal on the edge of the box he appeared to onlookers to be attempting to side-foot the ball. Instead he got his foot under the ball so that it ballooned towards the net. Jonathan, aghast, hesitated a moment or two and then hastily dashed out to collect it. But then, just as he was about to take it in his arms, the ball swerved wickedly away from him because of the spin that was controlling it.

Despairingly, Jonathan dived full-length to try and catch it – and he very nearly succeeded. However, the ball struck his forearm and bounced away. Lee Shoscombe, alert as always, had missed

nothing of what was going on. His acceleration carried him into the box before anyone else could get there. For him it was the easiest task possible to collect the rebound, swerve past the prostrate Jonathan and slide the ball sweetly into the net.

Paul Merchant sank to his knees, praying for the earth to open up and bury him. Damian dare not look at Ian Venn on the touchline. The rest of United's players were simply stunned. None of them felt able to say a word, either in anger or despair. Like robots, they moved to their customary positions for the re-start. Because of their celebrations it was some moments before Rangers were ready for the resumption and the referee had to speak forcefully to them. Behind Jonathan's net a few supporters were actually dancing jigs.

It was in Damian's mind that the whole season had been blighted by defenders' errors but he didn't voice his thoughts. Instead, with both fists clenched he urged his players: 'Come on, come on, lads. That was just a fluky goal for them. We'll get a real one.'

When next the ball reached him he controlled it well, smartly jinked past a couple of opponents and then fed Stevie Pailthorp on the flank. With unexpected perception Stevie immediately transferred the ball to the unmarked Neil Dallimore. Neil galloped forward for several paces and then hit a humdinger of a shot. Although the goalie palmed the ball over the bar, the swiftness and the coordination

106

of the move were heartening for United.

After the shock of Shoscombe's goal the home team's fans were coming alive again and the volume of noise began to lift the team. Even Paul Merchant could believe that Rangers were still a long way from claiming victory. He put his heart into his next tackle and emerged triumphantly with the ball. United's new team spirit, inspired by Bryn Marsden, was proving to be a true asset.

As the first half faded away Rangers appeared to be concentrating wholly on defence. They hadn't crossed the halfway line for several minutes and whenever the ball bobbed around their box they tended to boot it anywhere that looked safe. Twice United got in good shots, one that just whistled past an upright with the goalie clearly beaten, the other that struck the crossbar and ricocheted to a relieved defender who hooked it over the touchline for a harmless throw-in. Damian was constantly going forward with his attackers and providing a lot of vocal encouragement. His instinct was also to keep an eye on Lee Shoscombe, especially as Rangers' danger man had been subdued since his goal. Like a professional assassin, Shoscombe was prepared to be perfectly patient until the real moment to strike arrived. For the present, there was no point in wasting energy.

During the interval Damian asked his players if they had any bright ideas for getting the equaliser but no one could come up with anything really original. Several of them remarked on Bryn Marsden's absence and inquired if it was known when he'd turn up.

'Bryn thinks we're good enough to win this one on our own, so I reckon we should do just that,' Ian Venn pointed out. It seemed a fair comment. 'Rangers are just hanging on like rock climbers. One slip and they'll crash.'

Damian nodded. 'If we can get one goal we'll get two, I'm sure of it. So let's go at them all the time.'

Some spectators came up to offer advice but most just wished United luck as they returned to the pitch for the most vital thirty-five minutes of their season. If they failed to score at least twice before the final whistle sounded then there would be no future at all for a team called Darton United.

Rangers seemed ready to fall back on defence again. Their coach was a great believer in luck and it was his firm belief that on this day the luck was all with his team. As evidence he could point to Lee Shoscombe's goal: scored because of one of the luckiest breaks imaginable. Moreover, his horoscope in the Sunday paper had stated categorically that he 'would have a lot to be thankful for at the end of the day'. He didn't know then that his daughter was going to arrive after tea to tell him he was going to be a grandfather for the first time.

With a quarter of an hour to go, the visitors' defence was still looking quite composed when, rather carelessly, they conceded an indirect free-kick on the left-hand edge of their penalty area.

It was a moment Damian had been waiting for since the match began. As the Rangers defenders took their time about forming the conventional defensive wall, United's skipper conferred hastily with Alex and Billy Sandford. After appearing to give his instructions, Damian casually edged backwards across the front of the box. No one noticed that his fingers were tightly crossed.

As soon as the whistle blew Alex, who appeared to have been intently studying the one gap in the wall, flicked the ball to Billy on his left. Instinctively, goalkeeper and defenders began to move in that direction. But Billy hit the ball hard and low way over to the right. It arrived exactly as Damian had wanted it to: controlling it on the first bounce, he took one step forward and then cracked the ball into the vacant area of the net by the right-hand post. The manoeuvre, devised by Bryn and rehearsed so many times by the players involved in the training sessions, had worked brilliantly.

It was Damian's first goal of the season in open play and it was United's most vital equaliser.

As if on cue, Bryn himself arrived, dressed spectacularly in gold-coloured trousers and a dark green sweater. Within seconds he'd been updated on the state of the match and he looked as elated as Damian felt. He signalled his support and urged his players on to greater endeavour. Unless they scored again, they'd be relegated and face oblivion.

Inevitably, Darton surged forward again at the first opportunity until Lee Shoscombe made a timely interception in midfield. With a swift change of pace he headed into United's half. Lee still had plenty of energy in reserve and he was going to make the most of it.

Damian, who was on the other side of the pitch, could do nothing to stop the progress of Tinacre's star player. But, as if utterly determined to redeem his past errors, Paul Merchant charged in: and he had never produced a better tackle in his life. His timing was impeccable and, just as important, he kept his balance as Lee lost his: so Paul was able to collect the ball and launch his own attack.

'Keep going forward, Paul!' Bryn yelled at him and those words registered. When, at last, he parted with the ball it was in the form of a pass to Billy Sandford. Billy, who'd been playing as well as anyone in the team in recent matches, skilfully played a one-two with Neil Dallimore, took the ball into the penalty area – and was thwarted only by a courageous diving save from the agile goalkeeper. Still, Billy had gained a corner for his team.

'Take a short one and then push it across the box,' instructed Bryn, who'd dashed down the touchline after noting the height of so many Tinacre defenders. It was a ploy he'd advocated in training but none of the team had remembered it . . . until now.

When the ball reached Damian just inside the

penalty area he kept it tightly under control and weaved past a couple of challengers. Then, with the inside of his left foot, he pushed the ball strongly into the goalmouth. It was Neil who showed the fastest reaction. Jumping forward and stretching out his long legs he just managed to get his left heel to the ball before anyone else could make contact, and stab it over the goal-line.

It was one of the least elegant goals anyone would score – but it was enough to win the match for Darton United. Predictably, Rangers tried to switch from defence to attack but they had neither the ability nor the time to snatch a life-saving equaliser.

When, at last, the final whistle shrilled, Damian felt elated enough to turn a couple of somersaults. It was the most joyous moment of his football career.

Before he could attempt any more gymnastic feats, Bryn Marsden and Ian Venn had managed to reach him to express their own delight and congratulations.

'I feel as if we've won the Cup – and yet all we've done is avoid relegation!' Damian exclaimed.

'Maybe that is all you've done – for the moment,' Bryn Marsden responded with a grin. 'But now Darton United have a real future. We've got something we can build on.'

A Selected List of Fiction from Mammoth

While every effort is made to keep prices low, it is sometimes necessary to increase prices at short notice. Mammoth Books reserves the right to show new retail prices on covers which may differ from those previously advertised in the text or elsewhere.

The prices shown below were correct at the time of going to press.

☐	416 13972 8	**Why the Whales Came**	Michael Morpurgo	£2.50
☐	7497 0034 3	**My Friend Walter**	Michael Morpurgo	£2.50
☐	7497 0035 1	**The Animals of Farthing Wood**	Colin Dann	£2.99
☐	7497 0136 6	**I Am David**	Anne Holm	£2.50
☐	7497 0139 0	**Snow Spider**	Jenny Nimmo	£2.50
☐	7497 0140 4	**Emlyn's Moon**	Jenny Nimmo	£2.25
☐	7497 0344 X	**The Haunting**	Margaret Mahy	£2.25
☐	416 96850 3	**Catalogue of the Universe**	Margaret Mahy	£1.95
☐	7497 0051 3	**My Friend Flicka**	Mary O'Hara	£2.99
☐	7497 0079 3	**Thunderhead**	Mary O'Hara	£2.99
☐	7497 0219 2	**Green Grass of Wyoming**	Mary O'Hara	£2.99
☐	416 13722 9	**Rival Games**	Michael Hardcastle	£1.99
☐	416 13212 X	**Mascot**	Michael Hardcastle	£1.99
☐	7497 0126 9	**Half a Team**	Michael Hardcastle	£1.99
☐	416 08812 0	**The Whipping Boy**	Sid Fleischman	£1.99
☐	7497 0033 5	**The Lives of Christopher Chant**	Diana Wynne-Jones	£2.50
☐	7497 0164 1	**A Visit to Folly Castle**	Nina Beachcroft	£2.25

All these books are available at your bookshop or newsagent, or can be ordered direct from the publisher. Just tick the titles you want and fill in the form below.

Mandarin Paperbacks, Cash Sales Department, PO Box 11, Falmouth, Cornwall TR10 9EN.

Please send cheque or postal order, no currency, for purchase price quoted and allow the following for postage and packing:

UK   80p for the first book, 20p for each additional book ordered to a maximum charge of £2.00.

BFPO   80p for the first book, 20p for each additional book.

Overseas   £1.50 for the first book, £1.00 for the second and 30p for each additional book
including Eire   thereafter.

NAME (Block letters) ....

ADDRESS ....

....

....